I0519558

Also from Second Wind Publishing
Novels by Lazarus Barnhill

The Medicine People

Come Home to Me, Child
(with Sally Jones)

Mountain Woman Romance Series

Lacey Took a Holiday

www.secondwindpublishing.com

Caddo Creek

Mountain Woman Romance Series
Book 2

By

Lazarus Barnhill

Beckoning Books
Published by Second Wind Publishing, LLC.
Kernersville

Beckoning Books
Second Wind Publishing, LLC
931-B South Main Street, Box 145
Kernersville, NC 27284

First Beckoning Books edition published
July 2013.
Beckoning Books, Running Angel, and all production design are trademarks of Second Wind Publishing, used under license.

For information regarding bulk purchases of this book, digital purchase and special discounts, please contact the publisher at
www.secondwindpublishing.com

Cover design by Tracy Beltran

Manufactured in the United States of America
ISBN 978-1-938101-65-6

To S.E. and J.S.,

thanks for the inspiration,

—L.B.

Chapter 1

It began simply as an annoying awareness: her faithful little car—her beloved ancient, midnight blue Toyota Celica—seemed to have a lot of trouble accelerating up the steep grades of the mountain road. The annoyance became wariness and swiftly dread as she noticed the temperature gauge, always pointing halfway between "H" and "C," was as far to the "H" as it could go. Despair came next as the car began to chug and lose power, threatening to stop altogether on the narrow, two-lane blacktop with mountain on one edge of the road and steel guardrail hugging the other. And beyond that rail, a sheer drop-off.

Then in an instant, all the annoyance, wariness, dread and despair she had been feeling melted away as she realized there was another car immediately behind hers on the road. It was close enough that, in her mirror, she could easily see the stony, impassive expression of the young man behind the steering wheel, his eyes fixed on her, knowing she saw him as he returned her gaze. As her Celica continued to slow, sputtering and jerking, the driver behind her slowed as well. And when her car died and she steered its final, feeble, forward movement as far to the right as she could without scraping the guardrail, the red-orange car behind her coasted to a stop.

In that moment, all the other forms of anxiety were overwhelmed with a sudden cold stab of fear. Koral was so frightened she couldn't act, couldn't think. She couldn't even free her mind enough to decide if there really were a reason to feel so scared.

The car behind hers made a rumbling sound. The driver revved the engine. Then, her eyes still fixed to her mirror, she saw him disappear to her left. He was pulling around her. He was going to drive away.

Koral sighed. She felt herself breathe again. She was still in a really bad situation—broken down alone on a mountain road, but at least the menacing presence of the hard-faced driver was gone.

Only he didn't drive away.

She recognized what sort of car it was. Her older brother had yearned for one when he first got his driver's license.

"I need a Camaro, Dad. They are the most totally awesome ride. I won't speed or anything."

"No sixteen year old needs a muscle car, son."

And now the muscle car of her brother's dreams, a rumbling, fire-truck red Camaro, had stopped in front of her little Toyota and was backing toward her. It was lining up so that its rear bumper would match her front bumper. The Camaro, older but clean and dent-free, backed to within a few inches of her car. She could see the driver's eyes in his rearview mirror, staring into hers.

Koral felt her jaw sag. What was he doing? What should she do?

She wouldn't allow herself to freeze with fear again. Rolling the driver's window up with her left hand, she reached down to the floorboard of the passenger's side and pulled her purse onto the seat. Swiftly she locked both doors and began to dig in her purse for her cell phone.

A movement from the side of the red car made her look up just as she found the phone and activated it. It was the Camaro's door swinging open. Nothing happened for an instant. The door stood open, but no one emerged.

She glanced to the dashboard of her phone, seeing the simple "X" and terse message, "NO SERVICE."

What now? The phone was also a camera. She tabbed on the camera function and held the phone to her left ear, turning her head so it appeared she was looking off the side of the mountain and talking on the phone. Whatever happened next, at the very least she could take photos.

The driver got out of the Camaro. He stepped onto the road and closed his door.

Her face turned to the side, Koral followed his movements from the corner of her eye. She would try to remember everything about him.

He was very nearly her age—twenty-three—or a year or two older perhaps. He was fair, blue-eyed with a shock of thick dark blonde hair, just shorter than the bob cut of her own chocolate-brown hair. He was not especially tall, maybe only 5'10", a good four or five inches taller than she was. He was lean. Koral was thin, but this young man—his expression casual, almost disinterested, as he came toward her—had a hard, muscled look to him.

"Huh," she whispered. "Muscle car. Muscle boy."

There were two more things she noted about him as he began to walk. First, he had a distinct limp, one that made her wonder if she might be able to outrun him. And, second, he seemed vaguely familiar to her.

She intentionally looked away from him, actuating the camera button repeatedly. She told herself not to show fear, but rather to exude calmness.

Then she heard a mechanical popping sound. She looked forward to see him raising the trunk of the Camaro. It was the trunk hatch, but it opened into the cabin of the car. She could see orange steel bars, cage-like, anchored in the trunk and running upward around the roof. The driver was taking out some piece of equipment, something that looked like a harness. As he turned toward her, she realized he was going to attach it to the bumper of her car.

She waved frantically with her free hand and shook her head. The young man saw her and stopped. As he gazed at her, she turned away from him again.

There was a thud as he dropped the harness on the road and walked slowly to the driver's door. He was standing there, she knew, hands on hips, watching her. She continued to stare into the emptiness on the other side of the guardrail, the dead phone pressed against her ear and her heart fluttering in her throat.

He tapped on her window. Koral glanced over her shoulder at him. She pointed to her phone with her free hand and made the "okay" sign. He was close enough now that she could see his smooth, strong face clearly. His expression, more than anything, was one of impatience. Then she heard him speak.

"You can go on pretending all you want to, but there's no cell signal up here on the mountain, Miss Walker."

Her jaw dropped again. She turned toward him and rolled down the window an inch.

"How do you know my name?"

He gave a swift nod. "Because I sit behind you in your floral microbiology class."

She rolled the window down all the way. "That's where I've seen you."

3

"You want some help, don't you?"

"Well, my car stopped. Something's wrong with it."

Again he nodded. "Water pump, I'm guessing. I've been following you up the mountain, and you were losing coolant for four or five miles."

"Why didn't you honk or something?"

"Would you have stopped?" When she didn't answer, he said, "You can't sit here in the road like this. Somebody's going to come around the curve in a bobtail and knock you off the mountain." He started back toward the front of her car.

She leaned out the driver's window, calling after him. "What are you going to do?"

He was down on one knee, hooking something under her bumper. "My cousin has a wrecking yard and garage a few miles up. I'll tow you there." There was the rapid clicking sound of something being cinched tight.

"Can he fix it?"

"Oh, yes." The boy pulled chains out of the back of the Camaro and disappeared from her view as he fastened them to both vehicles.

"Will he be expensive?"

His eyes appeared, gazing along the line of the Toyota's hood at her. "You got a choice?" He stood and stepped across the hitch assembly. "I wouldn't worry about the repair bill, Miss Walker. I expect you won't even be able to pay my towing bill." Hands on hips, he said, "Put it in neutral and make sure the handbrake is off."

When she had done as she was told, she looked up to see him still staring at her. He shrugged. What was she missing?

"Lots of folks find that being towed up a winding road makes them carsick." He gestured toward his Camaro. "You could ride up here and be sociable."

Wordlessly she took her purse and opened the door. She felt immensely self-conscious, conspicuous, as she walked before him around the front of his car to the passenger's side. He seemed to make a point of observing her—her white long-sleeved pullover, worn blue jeans and hiking shoes—as closely as she had observed him. When he was almost out of her field of vision, she caught a glimpse of a quick grin.

The interior of the Camaro was roomy and clean and had a slightly oily smell. The bucket seats were some sort of plush fabric and very comfortable. There was no backseat, only an open expanse stretching all the way to the trunk hatch. Strapped down neatly along the sides were toolboxes and blankets and strange devices she had never seen before.

The boy reached behind her seat and pulled an odd-looking black seatbelt over her head. "Strap yourself into the harness. Pull down there and there. It doesn't self-adjust."

The throb of the engine coming to life startled her, not from the loudness of it, but the power. Vibrations coursed through her for a few seconds. The gear shifter was on the floor rather than the steering column, and it was a gleaming chrome blade instead of a round lever. It made a clicking sound as he slid it into place, and the car began to creep forward.

"So this is why my brother wanted one," she whispered.

They looked back simultaneously at the Toyota as it silently straightened and rolled behind them. Their eyes met as they faced the road before them.

"So what is your name?"

"H. L. Truett."

"Oh. So you're 'Mr. Truett' who sits at the back of microbiology and knows all the answers."

"And you are 'Miss Walker,' teacher's pet, who comes in at the last minute and sits right in front of the professor." The rumbling of the Camaro eased momentarily as he changed gears and began to pick up speed. "What exactly are you doing up here on the mountain?"

"I'm working on a course project for my botanical diversity class. I'm studying differences in *cornus florida* by geographical region and elevation."

"Oh, dogwoods. Yeah. Well, the dogwoods are in bloom up here right now, and they should be easy to find. This has been a good spring for them."

"My real interest has to do with their susceptibility to disease, based on those factors."

"Think you can track down and cure the blight? Is there a Ph.D. waiting for you there? Then are you going to teach?"

"Maybe .... What about you, Mr. Truett? What are you going to do with your Master's Degree?"

"I'm an undergrad."

She straightened. "No you're not. That's a graduate-level course. We have plenty of doctoral students in there."

"I'm a second-semester junior working on my B.S." He faced her. "I completed all my undergraduate biology courses and got special permission to take graduate-level classes."

The road curved and dipped before them precipitously and then rose again rapidly twisting in one direction and then another.

"Aren't you glad you're not sitting back there in your car?"

She studied his profile. He was not, she decided, a man who feigned the abundant masculinity, ease, and confidence he possessed. Those were simply expressions of who he was. She found him unique … and puzzling.

"What are you doing on the mountain, Mr. Truett?"

He smiled. "My mountain … part of it, anyway. I live up here and commute down to Fayetteville for school."

"That's, like, an hour one way."

He patted the dash of his Camaro. "Good car."

"Oh, so is mine. I've had it since I was in high school, and this is the first time it's broken down." She looked out the back window at her Celica. "I just hope your mechanic can fix it."

"Well, you really don't have to worry about that. My cousin Marvin can fix anything with wheels or an engine. He helped me rebuild 'Darlene' here."

"'Darlene?' Your car is named 'Darlene'?"

"Yeah."

"Where'd you come up with that?"

A smile erupted—unintentional, but broad and revealing straight rows of teeth. "Marvin chose it. His first wife was named Darlene." He glanced in the mirrors and down-shifted. "She was smooth, good in curves, had a few miles on her and faster than you could imagine. 'Darlene' just seemed appropriate." When she didn't respond, he continued, "Anyway, the other issue with your car is how much is wrong with it. A car that old has a lot of mechanical parts ready to wear out."

"Your car is older than mine."

"The body and frame are thirty years old. Everything else is new or rebuilt."

"You just like working on cars? Is that why you need a muscle car?"

6

He smiled. "I probably wouldn't be critical of a fellow and his car when they just rescued you and your worn-out jalopy from a dangerous mountain road, Miss Walker."

She stared straight ahead, composing her thoughts. "Koral. Please call me Koral. And I don't mean to sound ungrateful. I'm very grateful …. So, may I ask why an undergraduate student is taking master's level botany courses? I mean, just to be sociable."

"Horticulture. My family has always raised crops on the mountain."

"Really? What kind?"

He chuckled. "Well, I'm going to raise trees. I'm trying to graft fruit and nut trees that can withstand some of our more brutal winters. Might also put in some vineyards with different vines, *vitis vinifer,* for European varietals. Maybe some berry vines."

"That sounds very worthwhile, Mr. Truett. Why did you laugh when I asked?"

He seemed to think over his answer carefully. "My grandpa and great-granddaddy raised corn in the valleys and on the west- and south-facing slopes."

"Well, that makes sense."

"Uh-huh. They used it to make moonshine." He faced her. "They were bootleggers up on Caddo Creek, the stream that runs down our mountain. Now my daddy's interest in agriculture was somewhat different. He farmed in the narrow swales and overhangs and raised marijuana."

Her jaw dropped. " … Marijuana?"

"Yep. That's part of the reason he's in the penitentiary."

"Part of the reason? There's more to it than raising dope?"

"Yeah." The road leveled off a bit and widened. "He got cornered by some government men and shot up some guys. Didn't kill anybody. See there?" He pointed to a narrow drive that led into a copse of maples and up the steep incline of the mountain. "That's the entrance to my property."

She turned his words over in her thoughts. He might be teasing her, trying to make fun of a gullible grad student. He seemed guileless to her, though. Sincere. Was she foolish for trusting him?

"Your great-grandfather and grandfather were bootleggers. Your father grew marijuana. But you have broken away from your family's tradition, I take it?"

"Well … depends on how much money there is in peaches and pecans, I suppose. We'll have to see, won't we?" He glanced at her. "What about you, Miss Koral Walker? Is your daddy in jail?"

"Hardly. My father is a colonel in the U.S. Army."

"Do tell. Where is he stationed?"

"Right now? He's pushing paper in Washington, D.C. I think he'll retire in the next couple years."

"Is that your home? Virginia? Maryland?"

"Not really. I guess my parents would call California home. My dad has been in the military as long as my brother and I have been alive. We've moved around quite a bit. When I was about twelve or thirteen, we were stationed in the mountains along the Arkansas-Oklahoma border. That's when I fell in love with this part of the country."

He nodded. "So let me take a wild guess. You dad was stationed in Germany and met your mom over there and married her."

For the second time in five minutes, this stranger had totally stunned her by knowing something about her. A frightened part of her wanted to tell him to stop the car so she could leap out and run. Another part was hugely curious.

"How could you possibly know that?"

A satisfied smile crossed his face. "So I was right. It's your eyes and hair … blue eyes and dark hair. German traits. That and the oval face and turned-up nose. Very German."

"Yes. My mother is from Heidelberg. So were you in the Army? Were you stationed there?"

"No. I was a Marine. I spent a couple months in a U.S. military hospital there. The civilian employees were all Germans, and I got to spend some time moving around the countryside."

"Why were you in the hospital?"

He shrugged. "I was wounded. Why else would you be in a hospital?"

Koral sat, thinking over his words, remembering his limp. Perhaps he didn't want to discuss his injuries, like so many veterans she had met.

"It's sort of ironic to me," she said, "that my mother is German, and my brother and I were born there; but of all the places we've lived, I've never been back. I have no idea what it's like."

"Well, you'll have to go back there someday. Write your

dissertation on the differences between American and European flora
.... If you like this place, you'll love the *Schwarz Wald.*"

"*Schwarz Wald*? What's that?"

"The Black Forest. It's magnificent." He shifted slightly in the driver's seat. "Now me, on the other hand, I'm the guy who has only lived one place in all his life. When you ask me where my home is, I say right away, 'Caddo Creek.' I'd love to have traveled all over like you. Well, here we are."

The road had leveled out and on the passenger's side there was a storage area of about a quarter-mile square. It was surrounded by a hurricane fence with wooden slats in the links that effectively concealed the rows of junk cars behind it. In the center of the property was a corrugated metal building adorned with a hand-painted sign: "Truett Garage & Salvage."

As they pulled slowly toward the wide, dark opening into the building, a fellow walked out of the cavernous doors toward them. He was taller and several years older than her driver. He wore tan coveralls ... that did a poor job of concealing his sizeable gut ... with the sleeves cut out, a formerly red University of Arkansas hat and bulbous leather work boots, long worn smooth. He was holding some sort of L-shaped wrench in his hand by its short end and twirling it so that, when the engine of the Camaro died, she could hear it make a languorous clicking. And the man was looking at her.

It was only when she opened her door to get out—following the lead of the boy—that she noticed a massive brown-black dog lying near the open garage door. Clearly the dog was not chained. In fact, he wasn't even wearing a collar. His attention, apart from a casual glance in her direction, was upon a large bone he was gnawing.

The mechanic addressed her rescuer. "Hey, Four. Who's your friend?"

"I don't think she wants to be known as my friend. This is Miss Koral Walker. I have a class with her down in Fayetteville three times a week. Miss Walker, this is my cousin Marvin I was telling you about. She was coming up here today to study dogwood trees and her Toyota there broke down."

"What's wrong with it?"

"Water pump, I think. It was losing antifreeze most of the way up the mountain."

"Yeah. If the hose busted, it would have blew out all at once."

He leaned the long end of the wrench against his neck. " 'Course, if the water pump is gone, chances are it was the fan clutch went bad and wallered it out."

Koral heard herself speak. "How much is this going to cost me?"

"How much you got?" Marvin asked and laughed as if his question had been truly funny.

He walked to the space between the vehicles and stood watching as the boy unhooked them. Twirling the wrench noisily, he leaned back, surveying the Celica, Koral's precious, beloved car. He thumped the front tire with his nasty boot.

"What all do you want me to do with this heap?"

"Hello!" she said insistently. "I'm standing right here. Why aren't you asking me what I want done?"

The younger man—still on one knee—dropped a safety chain and the harness inside the trunk of his car, looked up at her and spoke. "Okay, Koral Walker. What do you want done?"

She stared at them. They returned her gaze.

"Well, I want it fixed."

The boy pulled off the other chain and threw it into the back of his Camaro. "She ain't got no money. She just needs to be able to drive it down the mountain to Fayetteville and to be able to stop it when she gets there." He stood and dusted his hands. "How long?"

Marvin tapped his wrench against the hood of her car. "I got a fan clutch will work on this model. I'm going to have to call in the water pump." He screwed up his face in thought. "Might be tomorrow before I can get it."

"Tomorrow?" Her tone was just to the anxious side of outrage.

He ignored her as he told the mechanic what he wanted done. "Well, if you will, get it running, check the brakes and fluids, and the belts, I guess."

Marvin nodded toward her. "Are you going to take Miss Delightful back down to Fayetteville?"

"Oh, hell, no. I got class in the morning down there, and I'm not making two trips."

"Well, what are you going to do with her?"

Koral found it surreal to stand before them and listen to these two strange men casually making decisions about her life.

"Well, she's not too big," her rescuer said, "but probably too big to stuff her in her trunk overnight."

10

"Could just leave her out here. She can spend the night guarding the place with Roscoe."

At the sound of his name, the giant dog looked up from the bone. He licked his nose and worked his mouth a couple times and began to gnaw again.

The boy stood, hands on his hips as was his way, regarding the dog. "Seeing old Roscoe makes me know it's about lunchtime. Think I'll take Miss Walker over to Trudy's and get her fed."

"All right then." Marvin started back toward the garage. "I'll call over there and let you know what I figure out about the car." He motioned to Koral. "Set your brake, will you, honey?"

"Honey?"

"While you're at it, Miss Walker—" her rescuer slammed his trunk. "—you might take the personal stuff you're going to need with you."

She pulled her backpack and jacket out of the back seat of the Toyota, trying to understand what she was feeling. Certainly she felt indignant. The big man was as much a chauvinist as any of the old-school soldiers to whom her father had introduced her through the years. The younger man seemed to delight in teasing her—and to have an uncanny sense of what she found annoying. She also felt tremendous relief. Whatever indignities were being heaped upon her, at least she was safe and her needs were being provided. Then, too, she also felt a strange thrill, an excitement as if she were beginning an adventure, the outcome of which would be totally unpredictable.

The engine was running when she slid into the Camaro and buckled the harness. The dog stopped chewing and watched her roll down the passenger window and lean her arm on the frame.

"I thought junkyard dogs were supposed to be all mean."

"Go over there and try to take that bone away from him. Let's see what he does."

They pulled onto the blacktop road, headed further up the mountain. She wondered why he seemed to be driving faster and realized it was because they weren't towing her car.

"Now where is it exactly you're taking me?"

"Trudy's. Marvin's wife owns a diner a few miles farther up. People come from all over to eat there. She can cook lights out."

"Wait a minute. Your cousin's wife is named Trudy Truett?"

"That's right."

"Well, I hope I'm not insulting you when I say that Cousin Marvin is a terrible redneck."

"You mean he's 'terribly redneck.' We are all rednecks, Koral Walker. Some more than others. Marvin, however, is the worst ... or the most. I have to say that his second wife has had a mellowing effect on him, though. Used to be he was vulgar with the customers—even the ladies. He would drink beer and belch in your face while he was talking to you. He had a huge rebel flag in the back of his shop but Trudy changed all that. She even made him take down the flag."

"Really. Because she thought it would chase away customers?"

"No. Because she's black."

"Oh ... What was that name he called you?"

"What?"

"That name. He called you 'Four.'"

The boy chuckled. "Yeah. Well, my great-granddaddy—who I never knew—was Henry Louis Truett. His oldest boy, Grandpa, was the second H.L. Truett. Everybody called him 'Junior.' My dad, Henry, is H.L. Truett the Third. When I came along, Henry Louis Truett the Fourth, folks just commenced to calling me 'Four.' That's who I've always been."

She studied his expression. "Does that bother you? Being called a number instead of a name?"

He cut his eyes to hers as he answered. "No. Does it bother you to be named after a primitive aquatic proto animal?"

She straightened and looked forward. "I'm not named after a reef. It's a woman's name and it's spelled in the German way."

"I know how you spell it." He pulled across the road into a small parking lot. "This is Trudy's."

The diner was a gleaming, silver building meant to resemble the dining car of a train and only slightly larger. "Trudy's" was professionally painted on a billboard above the front door. Eight or nine cars were parked in the little lot.

"Lots of folks here for it not even to be noon. We ought to be able to sit at the counter, though," he said. "You can just leave your stuff in the car."

"Will you lock it?"

He glanced at her, as if to see if she were serious. "That's really not necessary here."

12

She followed him across the parking lot and up the aluminum front steps of the diner.

"How did you know?" she asked.

"Know what?"

"Know how I spelled my first name?"

He paused, hand on the handle of the door. "Must've seen it in class, I guess."

Four held the door open and she stepped up and across the threshold. The diner was bright and clean and small on the inside. Most all of the tables were taken, but stools along the counter were empty. As she looked around, the eyes of the people seated inside returned her gaze, looking from her to Four and back.

A thin young man in a starched, tan, slightly-larger-than-necessary uniform, sat by himself at a table in one corner. He glared at her—or so she thought, until she realized Four was the object of his gaze.

"Is it okay with you if we sit up here?" He motioned to the stools nearest the cash register.

"Sure. I guess."

Koral slipped onto a stool. She was looking around for a menu or a board listing the entrees when she heard a woman's voice—not shrill, but insistent—call out.

"Four Truett!"

A black woman in her early thirties, nearly Koral's height but a good fifty pounds heavier, burst through the swinging door behind the counter that opened to the kitchen. She pointed a huge wooden spoon, larger by a factor of three than any spoon Koral had ever seen, at Four.

"Did you bring me my book?"

He plopped on the stool beside her. "They don't sell books like that at the campus store, Trudy."

"Ha!" The woman tapped her spoon on the service counter the way Marvin had tapped his wrench on her car. "What about that other bookstore in town? That new one?"

He shook his head. "Ah, that's miles from the university. I never have time to drive all the way over there."

"Do you mean 'Night Owl Books'?" Koral asked. "It's like only two minutes from campus."

They turned to her simultaneously, Four with a look of irritation

Lazarus Barnhill

and Trudy as if Koral had suddenly materialized out of the thin mountain air.

"Oh my god! Are you with him?" She glanced at Four. "Oh my god. Did you finally bring a college girl up on the mountain?"

"No and no. She is not with me. Her name is Miss Walker. She came up here to study trees and her car broke down. I towed her car over to Marvin's and then carried her here for lunch is all."

"Hi." Trudy shifted the enormous spoon to her left hand and reached across the counter with her right. "I'm Trudy Truett."

She smiled despite herself. "My name is Koral Walker. I do have a class with your husband's cousin here. It was just a coincidence that he was behind my car when it broke down."

"Really?" Trudy leaned back, a skeptical expression flashing across her face. "Do you believe in coincidence?"

"I thought I'd bring her over here for lunch."

"What about my book, Four?"

He sighed. "I'm telling you, Trudy, the University of Arkansas does not carry romance novels in the campus bookstore."

"Yes it does," Koral blurted. And when they looked at her again, she added, "By the magazines and cards. There's a whole fiction section."

He leaned toward her. "Remind me again of why I helped you. Look, Trudy, I talked to my V.A. rep about this. He said, if I buy you a romance novel anywhere in the continental United States, I will definitely lose my veteran's benefits."

"You're so full of shit. You just don't want nobody to see you buying it, son." She looked away from Four and focused on Koral. "What do you want to eat, honey?"

"Well ... I was looking for a menu."

"Don't need no menu. Just say what you want."

"You know that salad you made for Aunt Eleanor? The one with cranberries and walnuts?"

"My 'Spring Delight Salad'?"

"Yeah. She'll have that with vinaigrette dressing and some green tea. I'll have a BLT, some fries, and a root beer float."

"All right." And abruptly Trudy turned and disappeared through the swinging door into the kitchen.

Koral and Four sat silently, staring after her. In a few seconds a thin young woman, wearing the same sort of smock Trudy wore,

14

appeared from the back and set a glass of tea before Koral and a float in front of Four. The waitress disappeared into the kitchen without saying a word.

"This is the strangest experience of my life," Koral said softly.

"I'll second that."

"All I wanted to do today was find some blooming mountain dogwoods. I just wanted to see and enjoy a little of the beauty and wildness of spring up here. I wanted to take some pictures. Make some observations. Fulfill my course requirement …. The next thing I know, I'm broken down on the road, towed by some—some strange bootlegger's grandson, who happens to know me when I don't know him. My car is hijacked and held for who knows how much ransom. I end up at a restaurant without menus where they get mad at me for trying to be helpful, and they order for me like I was a child. And the waitress cannot speak."

He drew a long, slow breath. "Well, let me tell you about my day so far. I'm driving up the mountain toward my farm, minding my own business, when this flighty grad student I happen to have a class with has a four-mile breakdown in her car—a car that's older than the Ozarks. She ends up stuck on the two-lane where some logging truck or chicken wagon is going to slam into her. I try to stop and be helpful, and she perpetuates to talk on her cell phone because she's too scared to know what to be scared of. Then she commences to take pictures of me while I'm—"

"You knew that?"

"Of course I knew that. She complains about money the whole time I'm making arrangements to get her car fixed and then torpedoes me with my cousin's wife when I take her to get lunch."

They sat silently. Koral took a drink of tea at length.

"This is good."

"You should try Trudy's root beer floats."

"Maybe I will." She took another drink. "I have to ask you another question."

"All right."

"That policeman in the corner. Why is he staring at you like that?"

Four smiled. "Oh, that's Skyler Blank. He's no lawman." He glanced at the thin, uniformed youth in the corner. "Well … I guess, technically, he's a deputy sheriff."

"He sure is giving you the stank eye."

"Yeah."

"You mind me asking you why?"

He shrugged. "He always does. Always has. When we graduated Caddo High, I went into the Marines. Skyler … didn't get accepted. He also didn't get accepted by any other branch of the service or by the state police or the Fayetteville Police Department. Eventually he did make it as a Caddo County Sheriff's Deputy." Four shrugged. "Poor guy's always been a little jealous of me. Today more than usual."

" … Why today?"

A hint of disbelief crossed his face. "Well, today I came into the diner with a gorgeous coed."

She stared at him, trying to decide how to feel … then how to respond.

"I'm not a coed. I'm a graduate student."

The swinging door to the kitchen flew open, and the server dropped their dishes on the counter before them with a single unceremonious word. "Here." She disappeared into the kitchen again.

Koral caught her breath. "Oh my god. This is beautiful."

"Take a bite."

The bitterness of the walnut was a perfect complement to the tart berry and slightly sweet, salty dressing. She took three bites before she spoke.

"This is wonderful."

"Told you."

"How did you know I would love this?"

He shrugged. "Like I said, Trudy cooks lights out. Whatever you got, I knew you would like." He pushed his plate toward her. "Here. Try one of these fat French fries. You have to season all that virtue with a little sinfulness, don't you?"

The fry seemed to melt in her mouth. She took a second one from his plate.

"What is that wonderful flavor?"

"Beats me."

She stopped suddenly. "No menus and no prices either. How much is this going to cost me?"

"I don't know." He took a bite of his sandwich. "Probably $6.50. Maybe $7.50."

"How can she get by without a list of meals, without having the prices posted?"

He shrugged again. "People know what they want. You tell Trudy what you want. She tells you if she's got it. Then, if you don't already know, she tells you how much it will cost."

"Why didn't she tell me the salad would be $6.50?"

"Or $7.50? 'Cause you're with me."

"What difference does that make?"

"Oh, obviously, all my friends have big money. They can pay even $8 for lunch without batting an eye."

She leaned toward him, her voice low. "I can pay for my lunch. I can probably even pay for my car, depending on how much it is." She straightened. "What would Marvin do if I couldn't pay?"

He rubbed his chin in feigned thoughtfulness. "Don't know. I thought I might pay for it myself and force you to become my drug mule."

"Drug mule?"

"Yeah. You know, I put dope in your trunk and tell you where to deliver it."

"I know what a drug mule is."

"There's a couple problems with that plan, though," he said. "For starters, I'm pretty sure that beat-up pile of junk you're driving couldn't even outrun Skyler over there. That and I don't grow dope."

Koral pursed her lips. "Just a missed opportunity for you, I guess."

He laughed aloud. For some reason, a wave of relief washed over her. She smiled, looking down at the wonderful salad.

"But honestly, tell me, Four Truett. What's going to happen with my car, and what if it isn't ready today?"

"Well." He followed a French fry with a sip of his drink. "Sometime in the next hour or so—hopefully, before we finish lunch—that phone by the cash register will ring. Marvin will be calling to tell you when your Toyota will be ready. Which, if I don't miss my guess, will be tomorrow afternoon."

"Is he going to bankrupt me?"

"No." He chuckled. "He knows you're a student. He'll make it as light on you as he can. The parts aren't free, you know … probably a couple hundred just for an aftermarket water pump and fan clutch. And you can't tell me your belts are any good."

She sighed, a withering, sad sound. "And there's nobody up here who I can pay to drive me back to Fayetteville today?"

He held up both hands as if motioning for her to stop. "Honestly, I have stuff to do. I can't take you down the mountain this evening."

"It's okay. I can call my study partner, Richard Mills. I think he'll come get me."

"Mills? You mean that long, gawky character who sits by you in class?"

"He's not gawky."

"Oh. And your boyfriend as well, I see."

"Well, yes. ... he is my boyfriend."

Four suddenly had a look of resignation. "Yep. Well. Not hard to find Trudy's diner. I'm sure she'll be glad for you to sit right here and study until 'Stretch' shows up for you."

"Do you have something against my boyfriend?"

"Nope. I have absolutely nothing against Dick."

"Richard! He wants to be called Richard."

"I would, too. You might as well use Trudy's phone here to call him now. It'll take an hour for him to get here."

A car rolled onto Trudy's shallow lot, pulling up close to the windows with the muffled rattle of gravel crunching under its tires. Four glanced over his shoulder at it and his face was transformed. He instantly acquired the same stony, impassive look she first saw when he stopped behind her on the mountain road.

"I want to thank you again, Four Truett. This has been unforgettable." She cut her eyes to the car that had just arrived, a dark brown full-sized sedan with tinted glass and several small antennae perched on the roof and trunk. "The only thing I really didn't get accomplished was any work on my flora project."

"Hey, Trudy," Four called.

"Just a minute."

As he waited, Four did not turn to look at the front door. Koral did, though. She watched the tall, strongly-built man walk up the steps and open the door. He paused for an instant, surveying the patrons, who—with the exception of deputy Skyler Blank—avoided eye contact with him. He was, Koral guessed, in his mid-40s. He wore a neatly pressed blue suit, a dark tan, and a conservative haircut.

Skyler Blank, she noticed, nodded at the stranger, who did not seem to acknowledge him at all.

"What do you want, son?" Trudy had come out of the kitchen, this time waving a spatula.

"On the hill out back behind your storage building, don't you have that nice stand of dogwoods?"

"Oh Lord, yes!" she exclaimed. For an instant her eyes cut over to the suited man standing just inside the door. "They are all in bloom right now and pretty as can be."

Four nodded. "All right if Miss Walker goes down and takes some pictures and clippings after lunch? It's for a class assignment."

The silent man walked casually between the tables toward the counter. Koral realized he was headed for Four, who seemed to be the only person in the diner unaware of his approach.

"Sure, honey. You make yourself at home."

"She's going to stay here waiting for her boyfriend this afternoon, and she can work on her project while she waits," Four said. "You can't miss him ... tall, homely and overdressed. Looks like he doesn't have a friend in the world."

The tall stranger stopped behind Four on the side opposite Koral. He leaned forward and whispered something to Four too softly to be overheard by anyone else. Four seemed to be contemplating for a moment, then, without acknowledging the man's presence, he nodded.

The stranger turned and moved deliberately through the tables to the front door. He walked out, slid into the driver's seat of his car—which, Koral realized, had been running the entire time—and backed away from the building. He pulled onto the highway and headed down the mountain.

"Trudy." Four took a big bite of his sandwich. "As always, you are a marvelous cook."

"Thank you, Four. I'm married already, though."

"Yep." He wiped his mouth with his napkin and dropped it on counter. "I want you to put Miss Walker's lunch on my tab."

"I already have."

"Thank you." He turned to Koral. "Please excuse me. I have to talk to a man about a pigeon. See you in the morning in class. Hope you remember me." He stood and turned to leave, only to lean back on the counter, his face a few inches from Koral. "And no, contrary to what you said, I don't know all the answers. I'm just really good at guessing what the professor is going to ask."

She and Trudy watched him walk outside and get into his Camaro. He drove down the mountain after the brown sedan. Koral shook her head. "What an interesting guy. I don't know what to think about him."

"Sure you do," Trudy replied. "You're just scared to think it." She looked back at her hostess. "Do you know who that other fellow was? The guy in the suit?"

Trudy's eyebrows arched momentarily. "That was the maximum lawman. That was Corbin Lester, State Bureau of Investigation. He's the man who locked up Four's daddy in prison."

Chapter 2

Koral turned off the faucet, pulled the big stainless steel pot out of the sink, and set it on the counter.

"Is this enough water?"

"Just perfect," Trudy replied.

"Okay, so how many potatoes?"

She sighed. "One for you. One for me. Two for Marvin. My girls will have one between 'em. And one for Four. That's six, I reckon."

"Are you sure he'll come?"

"Ha!" Trudy smiled. "No Truett man ever passed up a free supper. Four loves my cooking."

"He did rave about it on the way to your diner this morning. And I can see why."

"I don't have a garbage disposal in the sink, honey. Just dump the peels in the trashcan and cut the taters into hunks about the size of a half dollar."

A shriek erupted from the den of Trudy's little house. Two little girls raced into and through the kitchen and down the hall toward the bedrooms.

"Stop it, girls!" Trudy called after them. "If y'all going to be heathens, take it outside."

There was silence from down the hall, followed by giggles and the voice of the slightly larger girl, her tone coy and full of trickery. "Okay, Momma."

"How old are they?"

"Jasmine is eight. Sage is six."

Koral gazed down the hall. "They are beautiful."

Trudy snorted. "I take it you mean their appearance. 'Cause they are ornery …. Their coloring is very elegant, isn't it? They are what back in the day we used to call 'high yellow.'"

"They're lovely girls."

"Yeah. My mother-in-law was pretty much ready to disown Marvin for consorting with a black girl until she held little Jaz for the first time. Then I wasn't so bad."

"May I ask how you two, you know, got together?"

Trudy glanced at Koral and then looked down the hallway. "Just need to make sure little ears aren't listening. Marvin was married before, you know."

Koral, washing the potatoes before she peeled them, nodded absently. "Four said they named his car after her."

"Darlene." There was obvious disgust in her voice. "That girl played him like a fish …. Ten years ago, not long after I first opened Trudy's, Marvin started showing up for breakfast. He was as despondent, depressed, and disillusioned as any man I ever seen. All because of the way his woman was treating him. He would come for breakfast because she was coming home late at night—being out with other fellows and having a good time and not even trying to hide it. When he would tell her to move out, she would smooth -talk him into changing his mind.

"Then one day I come to the diner to open at five in the morning and poor, stupid Marvin is passed out drunk on my front step, blocking the door.—No, honey, you don't have to cut 'em that small. I'm just gonna mash 'em—so I somehow get his carcass up and back in his truck and drive him to my trailer where I lived then. I put him in my bed and drive his truck back to the diner. I expected to hear from him about lunchtime. Honey, that man slept eighteen hours!

"After that, he came around for breakfast and lunch every day. I sort of took over his life … ordering him around, telling him what to do. I made him put a cot at his garage and sleep there." She peered at Koral. "We wasn't romantic, you know. I was more like his momma, who should've been doing all that instead of me, by the way.

"Darlene, she got to missing him, and it didn't take her long to figure out what had happened. So one morning about nine o'clock—which was early for her—she came stomping into my diner. She stood there, hands on her hips, and called me out for messing with her man. I was already working on lunch and I busted out of that kitchen with a soup spoon in my hand—"

"You mean that giant wooden one you had this morning?"

"Oh, the flour turner? No, it was an aluminum spoon. About half that size, but still big enough to leave welts on you. When old Darlene saw me coming in overdrive, she must've thought I was crazy. She didn't stay around to talk. She turned tail. That was perfect for me. I laid that spoon right across her fat ass." She paused, giving her guest a conspiratorial look. "Not saying my own behind ain't pretty nice and plump, you know, but I never give another woman cause to whack it."

Koral giggled.

"Well, all this come second-hand to Marvin. He was tearing down cars at the shop when he heard about it. When he found out what I done, my god, he was in love with me. He brought me a wildflower bouquet."

"Wildflowers?"

"As God is my witness. I ain't making it up. Of course, he picked the flowers off the mountainside. He wasn't going to pay for 'em .... That night we was romantic for the first time. After the next night, he says, 'If we keep jostling your trailer, it's going to roll down the mountain. We're going to my house.' I found out he had gone over and boxed up all Darlene's stuff and trucked it to her brother's house. She was out of his life."

"So then you got married?"

"Well … I wasn't using protection. I should've known better. We found out before long—" She pulled open the oven door and slid in a casserole dish. "—I was expecting. I didn't know how Marvin would take it, but he surprised me. He wanted to get married. Of course, first he had to get unmarried from Darlene. Whole process took

awhile. We weren't actually married until after Jaz was born. Now let's turn the heat on under those taters and I'll help you finish them."

"If you don't mind me asking," Koral said, "as much as Marvin loves you, why do you want to read romance novels?"

"Honey, Marvin is a good man. And he is a hard man—if you get my meaning. And he loves me. But he ain't romantic."

"Oh."

Trudy sliced the potatoes with swift, adept strokes. She set the pot over a burner on the white porcelain stovetop and turned the fire on beneath it.

"No substitute for cooking with gas. Now, while dinner is en route, let's get your bed ready."

"You know, I don't have to stay tonight." Koral followed Trudy down the bedroom hallway. "I could try my friend again. I'm sure I can reach him. I know he wouldn't mind coming to get me. And he can be here by the time supper's over."

"There's no sense in that. It's an hour up the mountain and another hour down the mountain."

"Yeah, but I'm displacing your daughter from her bed tonight."

"What?" It was the voice of the older girl. "Who's getting my bed?"

"Jaz, honey, you're sleeping with your sister tonight."

"Yea!" the smaller girl cried.

"Why, Momma?"

"Because we are good hostesses, and Miss Koral Walker, the friend of your cousin Four, needs a place to spend the night."

"Well—" Like a gymnast, Jaz twirled and propped herself in the doorway. "—if Miss Walker is Four's friend, why doesn't she stay with Four tonight?"

The question stopped Trudy cold.

Koral gazing into the frilly, girlish little bedroom of Jaz, guardedly responded. "Because Four doesn't have a pretty pink girl's bedroom like this one for me to stay in."

Hands on hips, Trudy said, "You mean you aren't glad to share what you got?"

Still wiggling and gyrating, Jaz thought it over. "How long?"

"Out of the way, woman child!"

"Just one night," Koral consoled her.

"Jaz, darlin'," her mother said, "get what you're going to need. Your schoolwork. Your backpack. Clothes for tomorrow—take that green and yellow outfit you like. Socks and undies. Carry it all to your sister's room."

Trudy ripped the sheet off the little twin bed as Jaz gathered her things.

"I am sorry to inconvenience you, Trudy."

"Hey, this made Sage's day. She always loves her sister sleeping with her."

"I was really surprised that Richard didn't answer. He must've been in the library or somewhere they make you turn off your cell phone."

"Honey, do you still believe in coincidences ... that he happened to have his phone off just when you happened to need him?"

" ... Well, if it wasn't coincidence, what was it?"

24

"It was what's supposed to happen."

"Why?"

"You know why—so Four will have to take you down the mountain to the university tomorrow."

Shaking her head, she smiled. "You think fate is pushing Four and me together?"

"Don't resist if it is, honey."

"Well, what if I don't care for him? Should I tell fate to take a hike?"

Trudy stopped, the pillowcase half on the pillow. "Do you dislike him?"

" … I didn't say that. I hardly know him."

"You sure light up when you talk about him."

"So why hasn't fate pushed some other girl into his life?"

"Waitin' for you, I guess."

"Yeah, but, I already have a boyfriend. So even if destiny means for Four to have one particular person, why doesn't he have someone else in the meantime?"

She tossed the spread over the bed and smoothed it. "I asked Four why he didn't have a girl. He said, 'I couldn't do that to somebody I liked.'"

Koral snickered.

"He had all the girls when he was a kid. They just fluttered around him like bugs drawn to the porch light. Then he went off to the Marines and Afghanistan. And since he came back, he hasn't had any time for them."

"His wound … did he … is he—"

"Oh, no, honey. Nothing like that. He didn't get hurt that way. I think he thinks he is so messed up from the war that no poor girl should have to live with him."

"How did he get wounded?"

Trudy stood, hands on hips. "He was a combat driver. They had him driving a Humvee in a convoy. And the Humvee behind him, which had a lot of important folk in it, got hit."

"They drove over an IED?"

"No. Not a bomb. It was one of those rockets you shoot."

"Oh, a rocket-propelled grenade."

"Right. Four was the only one in his Humvee, and he could see they was going to blow up the other one, so he turned around and drove into the—what do you call them—insurgents. It was just as they was shooting and it killed 'em all and blew Four out his door. Messed up his leg ... thought he would lose it, but he kept it."

"So he was a hero?"

"That's what they said, 'a hero and stupid.' They had ordered him to leave the scene after the first shot. But if he had, a lot of Marines and folk would've been blown up. They were helpless."

" ... And he went to Germany to recuperate?"

"Yep. And they gave him the Silver Star."

She smiled slowly. "How about that?"

"Let me get you something to sleep in." Trudy said. "You don't mind, do you, wearing one of my nightgowns tonight?"

"Not if you don't."

"I'd give you some fresh undies, too, for in the morning, but everything I got would swallow you—top and bottom."

"Oh, that's okay. I'm hoping Four will get me home in time for me to take a shower before class."

"I know he will. You just tell him what time you need to be down the mountain." She headed out of the door. "Just a second while I get that nighty."

As Trudy walked out the door, Jaz flew past her into the room and jumped onto the bed.

"I just made that bed! You don't be jumping on it!"

"Yes, Momma." The girl's face shone with a conspiratorial grin. "You staying in my bed tonight?"

"Yes. Just tonight."

"You can't get in my hope chest."

Her jaw dropped. "Hope chest?"

"That's right. You can't get in it."

" ... You're eight years old and you have a hope chest?"

"Uh-huh. Want to see?"

"Sure."

Jaz jumped down and pulled up the lid on a wooden box at the foot of her bed. "See?"

"Oh, it's cedar. I love that smell."

"It was Momma's before she married Daddy. Then she said she didn't have room for it in the bedroom. She put it in here and I said it's mine. Momma says that's okay because she gave up hope."

Koral laughed. "I see. Well, there doesn't seem to be much in here but romance novels."

"Yeah. Momma lets me read 'em."

"Really? That explains why you're so articulate."

Jaz leaned on her bed and swung one leg back and forth like a pendulum. "What does that mean?"

"It means you speak very well. You know a lot of words and you use them properly."

" … Oh. I heard what you and Momma were talking about."

"What's that?"

"About Four. About why he doesn't have a girlfriend. I know why."

"You do?"

"Yes. I asked him one time and he told me."

"Really?"

"Yes. He said he has 'bad leg.'"

"'Bad leg?'"

"Yeah. From where he got blown up in Gan-af-is-stan. But I've seen it."

"You have?"

"Yeah. We all went swimming last summer, and I saw his leg when he was wearing a bathing suit." Jaz leaned forward and whispered, "It's not that ugly. I think he could get a girl."

Koral, suddenly filled with the need to change the subject, looked back at the chest of romantic books.

"Your mom can trade these books, you know … after you both read them. You can trade them at a used book store for some you haven't read."

"No . Momma said not these."

"Oh? Why not?"

"'Cause most of them have black marks on pages or they have pages torn out."

"Really? Why is that?"

"Momma doesn't let me read everything. She says she has to censor it before she lets me read it."

"Oh." Koral's eyebrows arched. "I understand."

Jaz turned her head away, looking out the door of her room. In the next instant Koral realized the child was focusing on the rumbling sound of an engine, only slightly higher in pitch than Four's Camaro.

From down the hall came Sage's now familiar shriek and simultaneously Jaz screamed, "Daddy!" And she bolted from the room.

Koral followed the girls to the front porch of the little house. Parked beneath an oak tree near the porch, she saw a massive white pickup with a built-in hoist on the back and the running razorback mascot of the U. of A. painted in red on the door above the slogan "Truett Garage and Salvage."

The driver's door popped open and out stepped Marvin Truett just as the girls got to the truck. Marvin bent down and the thin, agile girls began to climb on him as if he were several kinds of playground equipment.

"What did you bring me, Daddy?" Sage demanded.

"I didn't bring you anything."

"Nothing?"

"I tried to fetch you Roscoe's bone but he offered to bite me."

"Daddy, we got company tonight," Jaz said.

Marvin, his head bent far to the side on account of a child clinging to his neck, glanced up to where Koral stood by the front door. His expression was slight bewilderment. Peeling the girl from around his neck, he straightened.

"Well, hello, Miss Delightful. I ain't finished with your car. The parts don't come 'til tomorrow, like I told you."

"She knows that." Trudy had emerged from the house and stood beside her. "She couldn't get her friend down in Fayetteville on the phone, so she's staying with us tonight. And, by the way, her name is not 'Miss Delightful.' It's 'Koral.'"

"You know," Jaz added gleefully, "like where they put the horses."

"That's 'Koral,'" Marvin said. "Well, what about her attitude? You know my rule: no courtesy, no gratitude—no supper."

"You ain't cooking, Mr. Truett!" Trudy exclaimed. "Don't get me started on your attitude. I'm going to finish supper and you behave yourself. Girls, you tell me if your daddy gets a smart mouth."

"Yes, Momma!"

She leaned close to Koral as she opened the door. "I put that nighty on your bed. It's flannel, but trust me—it still gets a little cold at night on the mountain, especially if you're sleeping by yourself."

"Thanks. Need me to help with—"

"No. No. I got it." And she disappeared into the house.

"Daddy, you didn't bring me nothing?" Sage persisted.

"Well, depends. Did you girls do your homework?"

"I did mine," Jaz crowed, "and I helped Sister with hers. It was easy-peazy-lemon-squeezy."

"You helped her or you did it for her?"

"No. I just helped."

"Well, in that case I might have something for you for after supper—depending on how well you eat." He reached into the truck and produced a plastic bag with the outline of a small, square pastry box at the bottom. "And you two have to share with your momma and Miss Koral."

"And Four."

"Four?"

"Yeah. Momma invited him, too."

"Hmm." He closed the truck door and handed the sack to Jaz. "Hope there's enough for me. Darling, carry that to your momma."

"Yes, Daddy!"

The girls flew into the house. Marvin walked up the steps onto the porch.

"Now there's something else I don't understand," Koral said. "Your wife is the best cook in northwest Arkansas, and you bought dessert."

"No, I didn't, Miss Smarty-Pants. That's from my Aunt Eleanor, who is quite the chef herself, especially when it comes to sweets. She likes to make delights for my family. Trudy always makes sure I bring back the recipes, too."

"I see. So when will my car be ready tomorrow, and how much will it cost?"

"If you have a class in the morning and get up here early in the afternoon, your car will be ready."

"Okay."

" … I'm still figuring how much it will cost. I was adding it up a while ago and my calculator overheated."

"Right. Well, how about a rough estimate?"

He sighed. "Seriously, the parts are going to run a couple hundred. The labor is only a couple hours. The car is really not in bad shape. The belts and hoses were pretty good."

"I love that car. I take good care of it."

The rumble of another vehicle caused them to turn toward the gravel driveway. In a moment the red Camaro of Four Truett appeared.

Koral felt a wave of joy and excitement wash over her and hoped it wasn't obvious. The warmth in her face made her wonder if she were blushing.

Four pulled his car in behind Marvin's truck and shut it down. When he opened the driver's door and climbed out, he wore an expression of curiosity and some other emotion Koral could not read.

"Hey, Marvin," he called. "Who's your friend?"

They laughed.

"She's not my friend either. She got marooned on the mountain this afternoon. I'm told you're supposed to take her down to Fayetteville tomorrow morning for class."

"Oh! Somebody should've called and told me. I've decided to skip that class tomorrow."

Koral folded her arms across her chest with a frown of disbelief as he walked up the drive to the porch.

"Floral microbiology is such a boring topic," he continued. "I'd go to sleep if Dr. Hanley would just quit calling on me. That's why I decided to miss tomorrow."

"Next week is spring break," she said. "You have all week to catch up on your sleep."

He ascended the steps slowly until they were standing five feet apart, staring at each other.

She gave him a prim smile. "You cleaned up."

"Yeah, I don't often get invited for supper at Trudy's. Figured if I bathed and shaved, she might ask me again sometime."

"Not if I get my way, chowhound," Marvin offered.

"Thanks, cousin. See if I tow any more broke-down flatlanders into your shop."

"She hasn't paid yet. You're on the hook if she doesn't."

"I'm gonna pay."

"You damn straight," Four retorted. "What happened to Stretch? I thought your boyfriend was for sure coming to get you."

"Richard was in the library with his phone turned off, I'm sure. That's a nice place for research … for those of us who happen to be able to read."

Four considered her face carefully as he decided on a response. "Speaking of payment, it'll cost you twice as much for me to take you down the mountain as it took for me to tow your car to Marvin's."

"Why? You're going that way anyway. And it's all downhill."

"Yeah. But I have to put up with you a whole lot longer."

She felt her lips purse. "That's why I'm having my boyfriend bring me back tomorrow afternoon to pick up my car. Richard has my back."

"Does he happen to have your checkbook?" Marvin asked.

She followed Four's gaze to his cousin's sheepish expression. "I'll bring you your money, Mr. Truett. As for you, other Mr. Truett," she turned to Four. "Why do you treat me so mean?"

There was an instantaneous softening of his face. He looked down the drive and replied, "That's just how I was taught to treat city folks."

"No it isn't," she said. "You have perfect manners in class."

He stepped closer, leaning toward her. "Well, if you had ever turned around and looked at the back row, you'd see my ugly, hostile expression while I'm answering."

"I'll bet."

"Now before I go in here, I have to ask if Trudy cooked the meal or if you helped prepare any of this food."

"As a matter of fact, I did."

"Hmm." He rubbed his chin. "Wonder if I should risk it."

"Hey. After we eat," Marvin interrupted, "I need your help with some Marine stuff."

"Marine stuff?"

"Yeah. I got that new .22-250 last week and I need some help sighting it in. I can't figure out what I'm doing wrong."

"What range are you shooting?" Koral asked.

The men stared at her.

"What do you know about a .22-250?" Marvin asked.

"I'm an Army brat, remember? A .22-250 is a small-caliber, high-powered rifle. It fires a fifty-five grain round at around 3700 feet-a-second. Typically they are used for varmints and small predators, although the shock it creates will bring down a deer. A lot of states don't let you use a small caliber to hung big game, so you probably want it for something else."

Marvin nodded slowly. "Coyotes."

"Uh-huh," she continued. "The extremely high muzzle velocity tends to cause marksmen to sight in too low. You may have your sights too high."

Marvin turned to his cousin. "Speaking of raising your sights, I like your girl, Four."

"She's not my girl. She's a classmate." His expression was skeptical. "I thought you were all into flowering plants and trees."

"Well, I am. Vegetation doesn't shoot back, does it?"

"You know about weapons, loads and munitions?"

"Sidearms, carbines, and rifles, mostly. I was certified in rifle and pistol marksmanship when I was thirteen. I'm the best shot with a sidearm in my family."

The men exchanged glances again and Four said, "Well, for future reference, if you had packed a pistol with you while you were coming up the mountain this morning when you broke down, you wouldn't have had anything to be afraid of."

She breathed in through her nose. "If only I had known your history, I wouldn't have been worried, Mr. Truett. My daddy taught me never to be afraid of a Marine."

"Come eat!" Jaz had run to the door and yelled out at them. "Momma said 'Everybody wash your hands.'"

They filed through the front door. Koral stood in the hallway while the men washed their hands in the little half bath. Since she went last, by the time she had washed and dried her hands and made her way to the dining area adjacent to the kitchen, everyone else was already seated. In fact, they were facing her and staring in expectancy. She stopped for an instant in surprise.

"Come have a seat," Jaz called.

Trudy and Marvin were at opposite ends of the rectangular table. The girls sat next to each other on one side. The sixth and only remaining seat was on the near side at Trudy's end—next to Four. Koral slipped into her rickety chair silently.

"Okay, Sage," the mother said, "tonight it's your turn."

Koral watched as around the table everyone joined hands and dropped their faces, eyes closed. It was a strange sensation to have Four reach out and clasp her hand.

Sage spoke in a deliberate, exceedingly slow voice: "Come Lord Jesus, be our guest. And let this food from Thee be blessed."

"Amen!" Jaz exclaimed.

"Amen. Dig in," Marvin mumbled.

Handing him the big plate of pork roast, Trudy said, "I'm so glad you could join us, Mr. Truett."

"I'm just so proud to be invited, Mrs. Truett. And I'm pleased I cleaned myself up, seeing how you have other guests."

"Isn't your classmate just the loveliest thing?"

Four reflected silently. "Miss Walker is quite attractive … in a 'city folks' kind of way."

"Is this a universal characteristic of the Truett men, to discuss people as if they weren't even present? And what do you mean, I'm attractive in a 'city folks' kind of way?"

He furled his brow, as if sincere. "Oh, you know, like, for instance, a hothouse flower."

Her jaw dropped. "A hothouse flower?"

"Get your elbows off the table, Miss Koral," Jaz blurted.

"Sure. You're a botanist," Four said. "Kind of. You understand that some lovely things are fragile and can survive and thrive only in the most delicate conditions."

"That is true," she replied, forcing the basket of warm rolls into his hands. "Other noxious and useless plants, like goatheads, Johnson Grass or cockleburs will grow in almost any location."

He held a casserole dish for her to spoon out a serving. A smile flickered across his face.

"I just love intellectual discussions like this at the dinner table," Trudy said. "Why, listening to you describe your interest in hothouse flowers, Four, helps me to understand why you've been shoveling the manure on so thick."

Marvin snorted.

"Have you been shoveling manure, Four?" Jaz asked.

"Figuratively," he said.

" … What's 'figuratively'?"

Koral leaned toward her. "It means that Mr. Four is full of manure."

"Euuwww!"

"Okay, okay." Trudy's voice rose authoritatively. "Let's change the subject. We are at the supper table." She sliced the meat on Sage's plate into tiny bites. "Miss Koral, why don't you tell us about yourself?"

33

"Uh."

"Anything, honey: where you're from, what you like, why you're studying at the U. of A., what you're going to do when you graduate. Anything."

Koral shrugged. "Well, I can't really say I have a home. My dad is in the Army and so my family has always moved around. There are four of us—my mom was about twenty when she met my dad. She was working on an Army base over in Germany. Then there's my brother Axel."

"Axle?" Jaz said. "They named your brother after part of a car?"

"No." She laughed. "That's a common name where my mom is from. She had a favorite uncle named Axel." She put a large helping of greens on her plate. "I guess I would say my favorite place I've lived was where we were stationed for several years at Fort Gibson over in Oklahoma. It's not too far from here, really.

"Anyway, I wasn't terribly good at making new friends. And we moved around so much that I sort of quit trying after a while. When we got to Fort Gibson, I was about thirteen or fourteen. It was just after school let out for the summer, and I had lots of free time during the day, so I used to wander in the forest around the base. Pretty soon I realized how many different kinds of trees there were …. Wow! These are really good. These are—"

"Collards."

"They are wonderful. Anyway, I started taking plant books into the woods. I got to know deciduous trees and conifers, vines, ferns, lichens even. One day in homeroom when I was, I guess, a sophomore in high school, everyone was saying what they wanted to be when they finished with their education. I said I wanted to be a botanist. Most kids didn't know what that was. When the teacher explained it, a lot of them laughed. I knew right then I was better off with plants than people."

"That sure explains your boyfriend," Four said absently. He glanced up to see Trudy glaring at him. "Okay. Okay. I'll be nice. I'll quit with the rough stuff … although she can give as good as she gets."

"As much as you've bagged on her boyfriend today," Trudy observed, "you almost sound jealous."

"Jealous? That's ridiculous. You can't be jealous when you don't have any kind of relationship with someone. Miss Walker here didn't even recognize me when I first got out of the car today."

"I did, too."

"No, you didn't. You said I looked familiar." He turned to Trudy, as if pleading his case. "The semester is half over, right? For eight weeks she's been coming into class just before it starts, hanging on tall-and-gawky, sitting right up at the front. She always smiles at Dr. Hanley and he tiptoes around her like she's royalty." Carefully he buttered a fragrant roll. "And the way she dresses— today was the first day I ever saw her wear real clothes, stuff you can walk in the wild with. Every day she comes to class in these designer slacks and dainty little blouses and half sweaters that would never hold up on the mountain. I had no idea she could stand up for herself in a real world give-and-take. And I never knew until a minute ago she had any useful skills, like field-stripping a carbine."

He had been speaking faster and faster, and, when it suddenly dawned on him that all the adults were staring at him instead of eating, he stopped abruptly.

"What? .... Would you pass the potatoes?"

As Marvin handed him the bowl, he muttered, "She may not have noticed you, cousin, but it sounds like you sure noticed her."

Lying awake on the soft little bed, Koral replayed the evening in her memory: the conversation with Trudy, surprising Marvin and Four with her presence, the family meal, and all that followed. The events and interactions of the previous few hours were astonishingly vivid to her. She remembered the walk down the hill after the meal and how she had sighted in Marvin's rifle and left the men speechless with her marksmanship, at the expense of a half-dozen empty beer cans set 125 yards away. She remembered sitting in the living room listening to Marvin tease and play with his girls in their hour of watching TV, punctuated with squeals of delight. And she remembered the sweet buttery sensation of Aunt Eleanor's pie crumbling and tumbling in her mouth, the last family moment before the girls climbed into Sage's bed together, begging Trudy to read them a story.

Above all, the silent presence of Four was in her thoughts in a way she could not dismiss, in a way that prevented her from falling asleep despite the great weariness she felt. True to his promise to Trudy, he had stopped his teasing and provoking behavior. Through the few hours of the evening, he had been a quiet shadow in the background of the family's activities—observing, unobtrusive, fully aware of all that was happening—much the way, she realized, he acted each day in the class they shared.

When Trudy escorted the girls to bed and Marvin, fetching beer from his refrigerator, slouched on the couch and turned the TV to the sports channel, Four spoke up. It dawned on Koral this was the first thing he had said to draw attention to himself since their target shooting.

"Guess I better be heading home. Delilah will be looking for me."

"Delilah?"

He smiled. "She's Roscoe's litter mate. 'Delilah' just sounds so much better than 'Big-and-Ugly'."

Four rose from the armchair where he had been sitting and stretched. He took a faltering first step with his bad leg and then steadied himself as he walked toward the front door. She stood as well and followed him out onto the porch. They stood side by side, gazing out at the broad expanse of the Milky Way bulging from the black sky before them.

"Oh my!"

He nodded. "It's easy to forget, isn't it, how different the night is when you get to a place where there's no light pollution? It's spectacular on the mountain, isn't it?"

"Yes …. Breathtaking."

He sighed and turned to her. "When do you want me to pick you up in the morning, Miss Koral Walker?"

"Well, Mr. Henry Louis Truett, the Fourth, class is at 11. I'd like to get back to Fayetteville by 9:30, so I can have time to clean up … if you don't mind."

"Sure. I'll pick you up at 8:15. Do you need me to call over here and wake you up? Trudy will be long gone by then, you know. She's down to the diner by 5 a.m."

"Yes, I know. I have an alarm on my watch. But, honestly, I'm an early riser. I'll be ready and waiting."

"Okay then." He watched her, seemingly waiting for her to say something else.

She had the feeling, as apparently he did, that the interaction between them wasn't quite concluded.

"I want to thank you again, Mr. Truett, for helping me out today."

"My pleasure."

"And thanks for introducing me to your family. I really enjoyed them all."

"Well, you're welcome. They were all on their best behavior …. See you in the morning, Koral."

It had an odd effect on her to hear him call her simply by her name for the first time. She stood on the top step, watching him walk toward the Camaro.

"Night," she called.

She woke suddenly with a jerk, surprised that she had fallen asleep. As she began to drift back to sleep, she heard a muffled rhythmic sound. It was the slight, regular compression of bedsprings and with it stifled human expressions: excited breathing, slight moaning, whispered words.

Koral, eyes open, held her breath. She didn't want to move or make any noise. She didn't want Trudy and Marvin to know she was awake and listening to them making love.

The sounds Trudy uttered grew louder progressively, and the pounding of the springs grew slightly quicker. Marvin began to make a slow, rasping sound as well. Then the bed stopped creaking and there was a series of soft, high-pitched calls that came, she guessed, from Trudy. And then stillness.

Momentarily they began to whisper to each other. Their voices were scarcely distinct. Koral realized her own breathing had become light and rapid. She simultaneously felt excitement and guilt.

"Say, hon." It was Marvin's distinct voice. "You don't think she heard us, do you?"

Trudy shushed him.

Koral quietly pulled the flannel sheets up to her chin. Trudy had been right: spring nights on the mountain were cold, especially when sleeping alone.

Chapter 3

Koral heard the deep rumble of the Camaro half a minute before it pulled off the mountain road and up the gravel drive to Trudy's house. It gave her time to uncurl her arms from around her knees, stand up, and shake off the chill. She had been sitting, wrapped in a ball, on the porch for fifteen minutes when Four pulled up to the house—five minutes before the agreed upon 8:15 a.m. His car was delightfully warm and smelled liked biscuits as she opened the passenger's door and slid into the seat.

"Keep you waiting?"

"No. I just now came outside." She struggled with the belt, trying to remember how it latched and tightened.

"Want a sausage biscuit and some coffee?"

"Love it." She took the paper bag from him, holding it beneath her nose. "Smells so good. You're very thoughtful."

"Not really. Last night Trudy told me to stop by the diner this morning on the way over. She knew you wouldn't be up before she left at 5."

"I'm so glad there is a thoughtful person in your family, you know, to make up for you and Marvin."

"Ha. I'm very thoughtful. Considerate. Generous."

"Oh really?" She loosened the lid on the coffee cup. "You have documented evidence of this, or is it pretty much your personal opinion?"

"Oh no. I can prove it right here and now."

"Do tell.

"Sure. I'm letting you eat and drink inside Darlene. Most hitchhikers are lucky if I let them listen to the radio."

They pulled off the gravel and onto the blacktop, headed down the mountain toward Fayetteville.

"Wow. Why do I get such star treatment? You just feeling magnanimous because it's Friday and next week is spring break?"

"What can I say? You bring out the best in me."

She took a bite of the steaming biscuit. "This is the best in you? The way you constantly tease me? That's the best you have to offer?"

The question genuinely seemed to baffle him for an instant. Then he replied. "I don't mean to treat you badly. Honest. I don't …. It is sort of fun to tease you. I mean, what with you being a flat-land, city girl."

She dabbed the edges of her mouth with a napkin. "How many city girls you know can name the species of every tree in a square mile on your mountain?"

He smiled. "In a way that makes it even more fun to send you up, since you're so smart and all. But I really don't mean to hurt your feelings …. Maybe part of it is that the best defense is a good offense."

"What?"

"Well, here I am, an Arkansas hillbilly. I wandered into a classroom because they kicked me out of the service. I'm taking classes I'm not really supposed to be in. Maybe I feel like, if I pick at you, you'll defend yourself instead of noticing my obvious deficiencies."

Shaking her head slowly, she said, "Actually when I see you, I see a courageous veteran whose country is paying him back for his service by providing him with an education. I see a fellow with so much drive and intelligence that he has gone beyond the ordinary to take advantage of his opportunities."

He stared down the road. "Well, if I hadn't promised not to tease you, right now I'd say you ought to give up botany and sell bullshit."

She laughed, choking on her coffee.

"And while we're being completely honest," he said, "I'm just not all that fond of talking about myself. If it's all the same, I'd much rather talk about you."

A little jolt ran through her. "Me?"

"Yeah. What with all the jawing back and forth, I haven't had much chance to find out much about you."

"Oh really? Seems like you always know more about me than you let on. You knew how to spell my name yesterday and we hadn't even met. You knew I was of German descent. You knew I was dating Richard—"

"And that's another thing. I want to apologize for picking on him. I mean, he's your guy and I keep sending him up. He's not even here to defend himself. I won't tease you about him anymore either."

She studied him, her head tilted to one side and wearing a look of tremendous curiosity.

"Well, anyway," he continued, "I know you're an Army brat— nothing personal, that you are not only an expert in vegetation but also in weaponry—at least small arms. You are planning to save the planet from dogwood blight and become a biology professor. What else can you tell me about Koral Walker?"

"...Well, you may already know everything worth knowing."

"I seriously doubt that. I'm not trying to be nosey or nothing. We just have this one hour together here. So tell me what music you like. What food do you like? Do you go to movies? Do you read books? Not romance, I hope."

She wadded the empty biscuit wrapper and dropped it into the sack at her feet. "Now that you mention it, I don't talk much about myself either. In fact, I don't remember having a guy ask me just to talk about myself."

"Guy? I'm not a guy. I'm your ... colleague."

"I'm pretty sure you're a guy—bad leg and all."

"What?"

"Well, okay, let me tell you something totally weird about me. This should satisfy your curiosity about just how strange I am." She waited for him to say something cutting, or at least mocking, and when he didn't, she continued. "Movies? I like the old black-and-white ones. You know ... from the 40's and 50's. When my mom first came to the United States, she found out that she could check them out of libraries wherever we were stationed. Old 16 millimeter movies. She had a projector and everything. Then she discovered VCR's and discovered you could get a lot of the old movies on tape as well. That's how she learned English and she fell in love with the old stars. I fell for 'em, too." She glanced over at him. "Cary Grant. Stewart Granger. Clark Gable. Gary Cooper. Gregory Peck. I thought he was so handsome."

"Well, that explains that."

"Explains what?"

"You know, tall and ... lean."

"Oh. Richard is nothing like Gregory Peck. For god's sake, I also thought Ben Johnson was terrifically handsome. You know who he was?"

"The cowboy star? Sure. Why?"

"Well he ... kind of reminds me of you."

"Ha." A spontaneous, easy smile—the one she remembered from the previous day—broke across his face.

The mountain road had suddenly grown much steeper and the vista more breathtaking. She drew a halting breath and said, "And the women were so glamorous. Marilyn Monroe. Oh my god—Grace Kelly. Katherine Hepburn. Susan Hayward."

"Ingrid Bergman," he said quietly.

She studied his profile. "And they were wonderful together, the men and women. When I was a little girl, I absolutely refused to believe that William Powell and Myrna Loy weren't married in real life."

He nodded. "The Thin Man."

"Yes."

"Smart as hell, that guy. I remember those movies. Myrna Loy—hope I don't offend you by saying this—she had the sexiest little—"

Now she laughed. "I'm convinced a lot of those starlets shot their scenes braless, if that's what you mean. Censors watched them so closely. I think it was sort of a game to see what they could get away with."

"Speaking of which," he said, "I have to make sure I take this next little curve below the speed limit."

"Why is that?"

"There's a side road there that can't be seen from this direction. This time of a morning Skyler Blank sits there with his radar on."

"Skyler Blank? You mean that anorexic policeman?"

"Deputy sheriff. That's him. Most Fridays he's down here at the speed trap."

"And you know about it?"

"Everybody knows about it."

"But if everybody knows about it, why—"

"See. There's the nose of his Crown Vic."

The slightest edge of a large tan and brown vehicle protruded from a copse of blackjack saplings. As the Camaro eased past, Four kept his eyes straight forward. Much as she wanted to look back at the officer, Koral gazed down the blacktop ahead of them.

"Now then," Four said, "what kind of music—" He stopped abruptly, eyes fixed on the mirror. "What's he doing?"

"The deputy?"

"Yep. He pulled out and turned on his lights." He sighed. "This is about you. I know he saw you."

"Me?" There was a high note of disbelief in her voice. "I didn't break any law. I just grinned a little when we passed him."

"No. He wants to show off and act like a bad ass." Four nosed the Camaro to the small expanse of dirt along the guardrail on the mountain side of the road and stopped. "We don't really have time for this."

He put the car in neutral, set the emergency brake, and left the engine running. Looking out the back window, Koral watched the officer take his time getting out of his unit, stretch and pull up his trousers, and stroll toward them. Skyler stopped just behind the open driver's window, partially obscuring his body from the driver's view, in the manner of a trooper stopping a stranger.

"Kind of took that curve a little over the speed limit, didn't you, Four?"

"No, I didn't, Skyler. What do you want?"

The deputy leaned back as if Four had taken a swing at him. "Well, a little respect for starters."

"We're on our way to class and we don't have time for this."

"Late for class? Explains why you were speeding."

"I wasn't speeding. You know it. I know it. She knows it—"

"We weren't speeding, officer," Koral interjected.

Skyler bent down to look through the window at her. His voice assumed an unfortunate, unearned air of authority as he said, "With all respect, ma' am, sitting in the passenger's seat, you get a distorted view of the speedometer. Now, as a trained law enforcement officer—"

"Skyler, what the hell do you want?"

He feigned surprise. "I just want to enforce the law in this county. I don't want to have to pull lawbreakers, but you have put me in that position."

"That is so much horse crap and you know it. I done told you we're in a hurry."

"Hurrying down the side of a mountain is not conducive to public safety," he replied, still speaking with his slightly ridiculous air. "Neither is endangering the lives of innocent citizens so you can look important for your girlfriend."

She felt Four tense beside her. His face darkened incrementally, apart from his lips, which grew white. When he spoke, his voice had the strangest tranquility to it and an ominous underlying menace.

"First, don't disrespect the lady. She has a boyfriend in Fayetteville who is not me. Second, I'm not trying to look important. You are. And you're doing a piss poor job of it. Are we through here?"

Clearly the officer had no ready answer to the question. He took a half-step back, his hands on his hips. "I need you to produce your license, registration and proof of insurance at this time."

Four gazed down at his floorboard, his breathing slow and even, his hands resting on his thighs. Her mouth open, Koral watched him with a gathering feeling of dread.

"Skyler, this is your only warning. Go get in your car, turn around and go back to your hiding place. Do it now and it will be like this never happened."

The deputy shifted back and forth, his expression equal parts of anger and uncertainty. "Step out of the car, Mr. Truett, and maintain your hands where I can see them."

For an instant Four did not move. Looking out the driver's side window, Koral saw Skyler hook his right hand around a nightstick and slip it loose from his leather harness.

"Four," she whispered, "he's got—"

"I know. I see it." He leaned toward her and spoke softly. "I'm sorry about this, Koral. I promise you won't be late."

"Just do what he tells you. Don't get hurt. I don't care about class."

The instant he began to open the driver's door, Skyler barked at him, "Turn around and face the car! Hands behind your head!" He held the night stick in front of himself, ready.

Four stood and turned his back to the officer as if to face the Camaro, but just kept turning. In a single motion he ended behind Skyler, who, shifting his shoulders toward Four, began to swing. His back obscured Koral's view for an instant. Then she could see Skyler continue to rotate, the nightstick tumbling harmlessly through the air and the hand that had held it pressed between his shoulder blades. Four slammed the deputy against the trunk of the car. Koral heard herself gasp. For a second Skyler seemed stunned. Then he tried to reach around his back with his left hand to grab his holstered revolver.

"You grab that pistol and I'll break your arm, son." Four's voice was quiet.

He searched along Skyler's belt with his free hand, popped a button, and produced a pair of handcuffs. Bending the officer's left arm behind him as well, Four lifted him, and they began to walk back up the mountain road.

An even greater feeling of alarm spread through her, and Koral slid out of her seat harness and climbed out the passenger's door. She stood beside the car, watching Four slowly walk the deputy back to his Crown Vic.

"Four?"

"You can just sit in there if you want to, Koral. This will only take a minute."

"Miss! Get on my radio. Call for help. Any frequency."

"Shut up, son." He looked up at her. "Hey, as long as you're out of the car, will you fetch that billy club by my tire and toss it in his front seat? Somebody's going to find that and get hurt with it."

She felt as if she were in a daze, watching a movie from the inside. The nightstick he had effortlessly taken from the officer was lying beside the rear tire of the Camaro. She stooped and retrieved it. As she walked back to the deputy's car, Four was handcuffing Skyler to a rod that ran along the interior of the back seat. He glanced up at her with an altogether casual expression.

"Just drop it in the front floorboard, if you will."

"Miss." Skyler's voice was desperate, fearful. "If you help this man, it's aiding and abetting."

Koral shrugged. "Well, what could I do, Skyler?"

"She's got you there."

The handcuffs made a ratcheting sound as Four secured them. He slid into the front seat, pushing buttons on an instrument panel. The rear windows smoothly opened.

"He can't open them from back there," he explained. "Child locks."

"You can't get away with this, Four," the deputy called.

"And you can't do anything about it, Skyler." He was examining the radio and slipped the microphone from its clip on the dashboard.

"...You can't treat a law enforcement officer this way."

When she realized Skyler had begun to cry, Koral looked away from him.

"I will get even with you."

"You brought this on yourself, boy." He looked over his shoulder through the Plexiglas between the front and back cabins of the car. "I was obeying the law and minding my own business. You think I wanted any of this to go down?" He looked out at Koral. "Could you tell me the number on the fender of this unit?"

She stepped back. A dark brown "17" was painted on the side of the vehicle.

"Seventeen."

"Thanks. Now listen to me, Skyler. The only way you're going to save any face out of this is to keep your mouth shut. Don't say anything while I'm on the radio. Don't say anything when they come to get you."

"'Cause if I do, are you going to find me and hurt me?"

"I don't have to hurt you, dumb ass. Don't you get it? If you tell 'em what happened, they will kick you out of the sheriff's department."

"...What would happen to you?"

"Oh, they'd offer me your job." He held the mike to his chin. "Now keep your mouth shut." He keyed the mike. "Dispatch, this is unit 17."

After a moment, a squawk of static burst over the speaker and then a woman's voice: "Four Truett—is that you?"

"Nelda?"

"That is you. How is your Aunt Eleanor?"

"Well she's much better. Thank you for asking. She's through with the treatments and they say her prognosis is really good."

"You tell her I said 'hello'."

"Thank you. I will."

"By the way, what are you doing calling in on Deputy Blank's radio?"

"So, Skyler ran into a little problem here I can't help him with. Apparently he was experimenting with his handcuffs and accidentally latched himself in the backseat of his car."

"And why don't you just unlock the cuffs?"

"Unfortunately, Nelda, he seems to have lost the key under the car, and I don't have time to find it." Four leaned out the open driver's door and tossed the handcuff key under the Crown Vic.

"I see." The woman's voice possessed a hint of skeptical humor.

"I'm on my way to take a classmate down to school or I'd drive him to the station myself. Can you send somebody up to get him loose? He's just down from the speed trap."

"Is that classmate you're talking about the young lady friend of yours I heard about? The pretty girl you had at Trudy's yesterday at lunch time?"

Koral and Skyler glanced at one another.

"She's just a student at the university, Nelda. Her car broke down going up the mountain and I'm helping her out with a ride back to school. That's why I can't help Skyler out."

"Um hmm. I think Deputy Murphy is still having breakfast at the diner. I'll have him swing by and set Skyler loose."

"Thanks. Unit 17 clear."

"Base clear."

Four stepped out of the deputy's car. "You ready to go?"

"Are you just going to leave him here?"

"Help is on the way. Did you hear that, Skyler? Murph is coming to get you. Treat him right and I bet he won't even tell the sheriff."

Skyler glowered at him.

"Come on then."

"Is he going to be okay in there?"

"Nice cool morning like this? He ought to be."

"I just feel bad leaving him here."

Four looked over his shoulder and waved at Skyler. "Life is all about choices, Miss Walker. Deputy Blank chose to harass us without due cause. His choices put him in the back of his own squad car, shackled with his own handcuffs." He held the door open for her and closed it after she slipped into the passenger's seat. "Of course, the Good Lord always sees to it that some positive comes out of all bad choices." He climbed behind the steering wheel and buckled in.

"For instance? Something good is going to come of this?"

"More than one good thing, Miss Walker." He revved the engine and spun away, gravel and dirt flying back onto the deputy's car. "For instance, do you think Skyler will ever try something like that stunt again? No way. So he learned a valuable lesson he'll carry with him always. Then, too, all the deputies will get a nice laugh out of it. And—" He glanced at her and smiled. "—it means we can drive down the mountain just as fast as we want because the deputy assigned to monitor traffic is handcuffed in his own back seat."

" ... How fast do you want to drive down the mountain?"

"I promise I won't scare you."

"You mean 'again'? You already scared me once."

He turned toward her, studying her face. "I'm sorry I scared you .... I wish I knew a better way to have handled that." He faced the road. "I'll get you back to your place safely." His voice had grown quiet, the tiny note of joy that had been present moments before was gone. "I promise you I won't speed."

Richard was sitting at her computer desk reading and highlighting a textbook when she opened the door to her apartment. He gazed over the top of his glasses at her momentarily before looking back to the book.

"There you are. I was getting a little worried about you," he said in an unworried voice.

"Didn't you get my text message?" she asked. "I wrote as soon as I had a cell signal."

"I got it," he replied. "Sort of cryptic. 'Car broke down on mountain. Back in time for class.' Didn't explain much really."

She asked herself why she should have to explain anything but responded by saying, "My water pump died halfway up the mountain. It was sort of exciting and dangerous."

"Hmm. You make it sound more like fun."

"Well, I guess it was that, too." She dropped her book bag on the armchair and went into her bedroom. "I need to take a shower. And I have an errand to run before class."

Richard appeared at her bedroom door, one shoulder leaning against the frame. "Want me to come in with you? Wash your back?"

Suddenly the thought of showering with him was the least appealing thing she could imagine. "No, Richard. Like I said, I have things I have to get done before class." She found herself hurrying as she gathered the clothes she was going to wear.

"So you were stuck up there all night? Where did you stay while they were fixing your car?"

"My car isn't fixed. It's still on the mountain." It occurred to her that she didn't want to ask him help her retrieve the Toyota. "A very nice lady, a young woman who runs a diner, let me spend the night with her and her family. Her husband is the mechanic who's repairing my Celica."

"Do you trust him? I mean, you don't know him."

"Do I have a choice?" She pushed past him as she walked to the bathroom. She reached through the curtain into the tub and turned on the water. Glancing over her shoulder, she saw him lean against the bathroom door frame, wearing a thoughtful expression.

"Well, if your car is still broken down, how did you get back to Fayetteville?"

"I got rescued."

The water warmed much quicker in town than it did in the heights of the Ozarks. That morning she had washed her face and brushed her teeth with Trudy's spare toothbrush before the water got warm enough for her to realize she had only turned on the hot spigot.

"We have a classmate, the fellow who sits at the back of floral microbiology with light brown hair. You know who I'm talking about?"

"I think so. Doesn't talk much, but always right on target. Pruitt, I think they call him."

"Truett. He lives up there. He's the one who gave me a ride this morning."

She stood and closed the door. It surprised him.

"I'll wait out here. I guess."

"All right."

She pulled off her clothes and stepped into the tub. For a full minute she stood beneath the warm stream, head down, water running over her hair and down her back. Gradually she became conscious of rubbing the insides of her forearms against her breasts. She opened her eyes and looked at her nipples, dark and erect. She was thinking of Four Truett.

Koral played the previous hour back through her memory: the rumble of his car before she saw it; the smell and flavor of the sausage biscuit and coffee; the effortless authority with which he had disarmed the deputy; and the thrill and fear she had felt.

She recalled the silence that marked the rest of their ride down the mountain. Four had misunderstood, she knew, her reaction to the encounter with the officer. He thought she was afraid and angry. Instead, she had been feeling awe and excitement. She knew of no adequate way to convey to him what she was thinking and feeling ... and yearning. Never had she experienced the sort of thrill and desire that had gripped her in the last, quiet minutes of their ride. How desperately she needed to express to Four what he had done to her. Yet she had no idea how to say it. As they approached Fayetteville, it occurred to her that he might be repulsed by her. After all, he was the one with power and grace and ability. What in kind did she have to show him? As quickly as it had come, the fleeting fear was overruled by her overwhelming, irresistible desire to be with him, to know him in every way. And all the while, this strange new storm raged within her as Four sat chastened beside her, oblivious to what she was feeling.

As they had pulled into the outskirts of the city, he had spoken at last, without looking in her direction. "I just want you to know I won't bother you, Miss Walker."

"Bother me?"

He nodded. "I'm guessing this whole thing has been a sort of shock to you. I am ... an uncivilized kind of guy. I dwell among uncivilized folks, but it's no reflection on you. You're a fine person. Marvin will have your car ready this afternoon, I'm certain. Richard will follow you up to Caddo Creek and back down here." He shrugged. "You'll be fine."

She had faced him when he began to talk and had listened to him silently. As he spoke, something like a hunger began to gnaw within her. Koral knew beyond doubt what she wanted. She was unsure of how to ask for it. Never before had she desired anything or anyone so fiercely.

Solemnly she gave him directions to the student apartment building where she lived. When he stopped in front of her complex, she reached into the empty area behind her seat and grabbed her backpack.

"I don't think it's a good offense," she had said as she opened her door.

"What?"

"The reason you tease me and poke at me. It isn't just gigging me so I won't notice your deficiencies."

"Oh. Really?"

"It's a really good defense on your part. It keeps people from getting too close to you."

He had smiled. "Why would I want to do that?"

"If you had let me get closer, maybe I'd know." She got out of the car and stood. "You going to class today?"

"Well, yeah."

"See you there." She had turned her back on him and walked away.

Koral replayed that last moment of being with him again and again as she finished washing her hair and her body, turned off the water, stepped out of the tub, took her towel, and wiped the steam from the mirror to look at herself. Two things dawned on her in that moment.

First, she had broken her constant routine. Never had she gotten out of the shower to dry off. Always she stood in the tub until she had dabbed away every drop of moisture. Yet here she was, nothing dry about her, the linoleum beneath her pooling with the water cascading down her limbs.

Second, Koral had an expression on her face she had never worn before, but one she had recently seen. It was a look of slightly defiant joy. Exhilaration. Power. She had never seen that in her eyes or in the set of her mouth before. Where had she seen it? On the face of the boy. It was the look Four had as he walked back to his car after cuffing and leaving the deputy. And now it was her look.

"Oh my god." Her voice was barely audible above the water spattering on the floor. "I have 'outlaw face'."

She dried off and put on her clothes and walked out to the living room. Once again Richard was sitting at her desk so engrossed in the text that he did not look up at her as she approached.

"I'm glad you're still here, Richard," she said.

Her comment seemed to surprise him. "Well, why wouldn't I be? We're going to class together, aren't we?"

"No, dear. Remember? I said I have to run an errand."

"Oh. Then why are you glad I'm here?"

"'Cause you let yourself in. That means you have my key with you."

"Yeah?"

"So can I have it please."

"Oh." He dug into his hip pocket and produced his key ring and absently began to take hers off. "Did you leave yours up with your car?"

"Nope. Got it right here in my purse."

He handed her the door key. "Then why do you need this one?"

"Because we're breaking up, Richard."

His jaw dropped. "What?"

"You heard me, dear. Is there anything of yours here you need?"

He was trapped in total astonishment between the reality of her announcement and the question she had asked.

"Breaking up?"

"Yes, Richard. Do I have stuff of yours here you need to take with you?"

"Uh, no. I have a couple books of yours at my place."

"Just bring them to class after spring break."

"Why are you breaking up with me?"

"I'm not that special to you, Richard. I guess I sort of realized in the last twenty-four hours that our relationship is built a lot more on convenience than romance."

"No, please, Koral." He stood. There was a note of pleading in his voice. "I don't want this to end."

"Relax. Half a dozen graduate girls think you're an absolute catch." She walked to the apartment door and opened it. "You know that cute little strawberry blonde in your organic chemistry class, the one who always wants to snuggle up to you?"

"Starla?"

"Yep. She thinks you are absolutely wasted on me. Go find her this afternoon and tell her you ditched me because I was no fun, and you'll be in her panties before the weekend is over."

Koral stood at the door, holding it open for him. He slouched toward it slowly.

Shaking his head, he said, "I've never heard you talk like this."

"It's a surprise to me, too."

He stepped into the hallway. "Well, then don't you think we ought to wait—"

"Nope. I'm sure."

"I don't know what to say."

"Well, then let's quit before it gets awkward," she replied, and closed the door.

From out in the hall came his muffled voice. "I'll see you in class."

Koral didn't answer. Instead she hurried to get ready for class and for her trip back up the mountain. She was going to see Four in class also and insist he take her back to pick up her Celica.

For some reason she found it maddeningly difficult to

concentrate on the usually simple tasks required for preparing herself to leave her apartment. She felt almost as if she were going through all the usual rote activities for the first time: drying and fixing her hair, putting on the little bit of makeup she wore, gathering her books. The entire process was clouded with thoughts of Four.

She found her larger backpack, the one she took hiking and camping, and filled it with the things she knew she would need. The weight pulled against her as she slung the strap over her shoulder and headed out the apartment door. Richard, she was glad to see, had not lingered.

The university bookstore was only a slight detour on the way to her biology classroom. And on the way, she knew, she would pass by a convenience store. She checked the time on her phone. If she hurried, she could make it to both before class.

It only took her a moment in the little store. She found a toothbrush to replace the one she had borrowed from Trudy and paid for it, along with two packages of peanut M&M's—one for Jaz and one for Sage.

It took her longer in the bookstore. She had to check the big backpack at the cash register and push through a surprising number of kids—buying clothes for spring break, she guessed—to the racks of paperback fiction novels. Koral had never paid any real attention to romance novels before. She was surprised to see them broken into subgenres: regency, contemporary, erotic, even science fiction. She started to pick an erotic title and then thought of the little girl waiting to read it once her mother finished. At last, glancing again at the time, she settled on two thick books, one contemporary and the other about the Old West.

Scurrying toward the science building, it occurred to her that, as was almost always the case, she was getting to class just as it started. This was the first time, however, it bothered her to cut it so close.

She made it through the door of the classroom half a dozen steps before Professor Handley, who in characteristically oblivious form, dropped the manila folder of his notes on the desk at the front of the room and began to write Latin scientific names on the whiteboard.

Koral's attention immediately focused on Four Truett, seated at the back in the row at the head of which Richard sat, his face stunned and disconsolate—and even more so when she walked directly to him and then down the aisle to where Four sat watching observantly.

She took the empty seat beside him and leaned over, her face inches from his.

"I need you to drive me back up the mountain to get my car after school. Can you do that?"

He regarded her with curiosity. "Sure."

"Good." She settled back into the seat, pushing her backpack against the wall behind her.

"All right, scholars," Dr. Hanley said. "Here are the scientific names of five spore-bearing ferns. What are their common names and distinguishing characteristics? How about you, Miss—" He glanced at the empty chair where Koral usually sat. "Oh," he said to Richard, "sorry. I thought I—"

The professor followed Richard's gesture toward the back of the classroom. He stared at Koral, seated beside Four.

"Oh."

She smiled. "I can name them, Dr. Hanley."

Chapter 4

Windows down and the engine pulsing as they began up the mountainside, Koral could feel the temperature begin to drop. She filled her lungs with the pure air and closed her eyes. They had been driving for thirty minutes and were halfway to their destination. If she were going to talk to the boy, it needed to be now.

She turned her head toward him, staring until he turned to her.

"You never told me how much I owed you for the tow ... and for the rides down and back from Fayetteville."

He looked back to the road. "Well, there's no charge. I was pleased to do it. When people have problems on Caddo Creek, we help one another out. Next time I might be the one needing the help. You'd have done the same for me. Wouldn't you have stopped if I was broke down?"

"Maybe. Would you have rolled up your windows and locked your doors like I did?"

He smiled. "No, but I might have taken your picture. That way I could say, 'Look who stopped for me, boys.'"

Koral shook her head. "Thank you for that."

"For what?"

"For joking with me. For a while there I didn't think you ever would again."

" ... Well, after this morning—"

"You misunderstood about this morning. You thought you had offended me, so you backed away from me like I had the plague."

"Misunderstood? That I scared the pee out of you? That was pretty clear. And since you brought that up, I want to apologize again for what happened with Skyler."

"Really? Why is that?"

"Well, I guess I could have handled that whole business a little differently."

"Oh. What do you wish you had done differently?"

He shrugged. "I could have kowtowed to him, I guess. Maybe I could have just said, 'Yes, sir. I guess I was speeding. I'll try to be more careful. Thanks for not giving me a ticket.' Something like that."

"But you weren't speeding. That would have been a lie."

"Yeah?"

"Well, then Officer Blank would think he could get away with bullying people. I started to say 'throwing his weight around,' but he doesn't really have any to throw."

"Skyler wouldn't really be getting away with anything. I would have hunted him up this weekend when he was out of uniform and pulverized him."

She laughed aloud and clapped her hands before her.

Four gave her a look of curiosity. "I wasn't making a joke, you know."

"I know that." She looked out her window. "What are you going to do on your spring break, Four Pruitt?"

For a time she didn't think he was going to answer. Then he said, "Tomorrow morning I'm going up on the mountain. May take my kayak and ride down the creek."

"That sounds beautiful. And then what?"

"Well, I was thinking I might go see my dad on Sunday."

"Oh. Where—Where is he—"

"Where is he in prison? Pine Bluff. He's a trustee in one of the units. He works as a custodian in the administrative offices."

Koral wanted to say it sounded like a safe, good place for his father. It occurred to her how patronizing that would seem. Instead she asked, "So do you get to see him often?"

"About once a month. I saw him a couple weeks ago."

"Oh. Are you going this weekend because you have extra time over spring break?"

" … No, actually, there may be an opportunity for him to get out earlier than he anticipated. I need to ask him if he wants me to take it."

"Wants you to take it? How can you get him out?"

He studied her face for an instant. "Same way I handled Skyler this morning: just waltz in and handcuff the warden and away we go."

"Uh-huh, and what if the warden is a big, burly guy?"

"I've seen the warden. He's a tubby little fart … about five-four, 250 pounds."

"Hmm. Sounds like there's not much to it. Makes you wonder why more prisoners don't escape."

Again he shrugged. "Too hard to find a job on the outside, I guess. On the inside you got free clothes, free room, three free meals a day, if you can call that eating."

"Do you really have a way to get your dad out of prison?"

"Maybe. Let's talk about something else."

"Like what?"

"Like—and I know this is none of my business—I take it you and your boyfriend had a falling out."

"Oh. That. Well, he's not my boyfriend anymore."

"I sort of figured that. I guess I was a little concerned that your night on the mountain had something to do with it. Like maybe I should have carried you back to Fayetteville yesterday afternoon."

Koral screwed her face to one side. "Maybe. Yeah. Yesterday was a big part of it, not in the way you might think."

"You mean he wasn't all upset about you staying at some strangers' house in the boonies without letting him know you were okay?"

"Kind of the opposite, Four. It's like he didn't notice I was gone."

"Oh. Well, I bet he notices now."

"It's really more like what I noticed about him."

"Yeah? What was that, if you don't mind me asking?"

She stared at him, unhurried. "I suppose I'd say we had a relationship that was mostly for convenience sake more than anything else. I guess I had all of that I could enjoy."

"So, as I'm getting this, it was your choice to end it, and you ditched the guy because he was too convenient?"

She nodded slowly.

"That doesn't make a lot of sense to me, but then nothing about you does. And, like I said, it's none of my business." He drew a deep breath and gripped the steering wheel. "So what about you, Miss Koral Walker? How are you spending your spring break?"

"Jury's still out on that one. Is there anything worth doing on the mountain?"

He laughed. "I'll skip the part about you being a city girl. You hate that. So the short answer is probably 'no'."

"Well, after you take me to get my car, I'm settling up with your cousin Marvin. Then I'm going to see Trudy. I have gifts for her and the girls."

"That's thoughtful of you."

"After that, I'm just not sure."

"Well, your car ought to be working fine. Marvin couldn't find all that much wrong with it."

"I bet he tried."

"No, he didn't. He knows you don't have any money. All he tried to do was keep you safe."

"Aren't they an odd couple—Trudy and Marvin, I mean?"

"Well … I would have never have matched them up. But you have to admit they've worked out pretty well together."

"They're crazy about each other."

"I guess."

She thought over her words and summoned her courage. "You know how you said something was none of your business?"

"Yeah?"

"Well, I have a personal question like that for you."

He glanced at her. "Yeah?"

"…Can I ask it?"

"Sure. Can I wait 'til I hear it to decide if I want to answer it?"

"Okay. Here goes. Why don't you have a girl? …. Or maybe you do and your family doesn't know about it."

"…You mean, like a steady girl?"

"No, I mean a wobbly one. Do you have any girl?"

"No. Why do you ask?"

"Clever, clever, but I'm asking you the questions, muscle boy."

"Muscle boy?"

"So you don't have a girl. Why not?"

Four looked at her. Then down the road. "They made me talk about this shit before they let me come home from Germany and muster out."

She studied his face. The golden hair undulating on his forehead from the wind was the only motion.

"You're talking about your war experience?"

"There's nothing like killing people and getting blown up to change the way you look at things. You can't come back from something like that and fall into all those high school love games again. Where am I going to find a girl around here who gets that?

Honestly, I don't think a woman should have to understand that. I wouldn't wish what I've seen and know off on anybody. And I sure don't want to hook up with a chick who's been over there and through all that crap. She'd be crazier than me."

Koral drew a deep breath. "Well, I guess Jaz was wrong."

"Jaz?"

"Yeah. She said you don't have a girl because you've got 'bad leg'."

"Ha! Well, I got that, too."

She leaned back against the seat and looked out the window. "Thanks for explaining it to me, Four."

He did not respond.

They rode through the switchbacks and dips of the mountain highway in silence. She recognized the place along the road where her Toyota had broken down and pulled up against the guardrail. It was astonishing to her how many things had happened and how many of her perceptions had changed in twenty-four hours. She wondered if she would find a way to stay in this new place and continue this adventurous journey.

A feeling of reluctance began to grow within her as she realized they were almost to Marvin's garage. She did not want the ride to be over. When would she see Four again? The ten days until their next class together seemed too long to bear.

They pulled onto the lot of Truett Garage and Salvage. Roscoe, the massive guard dog, was stretched out on one side sleeping and did not move. Parked facing the road by the open door of the shop was Koral's little midnight blue Celica, and from that open door Marvin strolled, wiping his hands on a red rag.

"Got you all fixed up, Miss Walker."

"Thank you, Marvin." She climbed out of the Camaro, pulling her bulky backpack out from behind her seat. "How much is it going to cost me?"

"A grand total of $137.45."

She stopped. "That can't be right. I figured it for at least twice that."

He shrugged. "I used aftermarket parts. And I might have cut you a little slack on the labor. My little wife told me to go easy on you. She really likes you. And my girls want to know when you're coming back to see them."

"You through with me?"

Koral and Marvin turned toward Four, who was standing in the open driver's door, leaning on top of the car.

"Yeah, cousin. She's ready to go."

"Uh, wait." She walked back to the Camaro. "Four, I want to thank you again. I really, really appreciate your help."

He smiled. "Well, if you see me broken down, Koral, remember to stop and help out. That way I can take your picture."

"That's twice you said that. Why do you want my picture?"

"Hey. You're not the only one who appreciates beautiful flora on the mountain." He slipped into the car and called, "Guess I'll see you after spring break."

Koral turned away, following Marvin into the shop. She forced herself not to look back as the Camaro pulled off the lot.

Against one corrugated metal wall was a disheveled desk with a lamp illuminating the clutter stacked across it. Marvin picked up an invoice book that teetered atop one pile and tore a sheet from it.

"Here's your bill."

She fished inside her backpack for her purse. "Do you need cash?"

"Naw. Just write me a check. You're good for it."

"Thank you so much."

He handed her a pen, gritty to the touch, and watched her fill out the check. She tore it off and handed it to him.

"And thank you, Miss Walker, for what you did for my cousin."

She looked up at him. "What did I do for him?"

"Well, you made him laugh and smile real happy and peaceful. I ain't seen that in a while."

"Really? You could tell a difference?"

"So could my wife." He pulled her car key from a peg board fastened to the wall and handed it to her. "Well, let's see if it runs."

They stepped out of the darkness into the brilliant April sunshine. Koral stowed her bag on the passenger's side and walked around to get in. Marvin came to her door as she rolled down the window.

"Hope I got your seat back in the right spot."

"It's almost right," she said.

The Celica started up as soon as she turned on the ignition. It hummed rapidly for a few seconds and slowed to a smooth purr.

Roscoe raised his head at the sound to look at her momentarily.

"Sound okay?"

"Sounds like new."

He smiled. "Well, if you're ever on the mountain again and you break down, remember one thing."

"What's that?"

"I'm the only mechanic up here."

She smiled at him. "Marvin, you are unforgettable."

Koral put the car in gear and pulled off the driveway headed up the mountain toward Trudy's. The Toyota ran smooth and straight, better than it had functioned in years. Koral wondered what Marvin had done to it. She knew his charges didn't begin to cover all he had repaired.

Leaning over, she rolled the passenger window down as well. Cool air whipped through the interior of the car.

"Where is that Skyler Blank? I bet my little hot rod would leave him in the dust."

Trudy's lot had a dozen vehicles parked around it at odd angles. It dawned on Koral that there were no marked spaces. She pulled into a spot between two pickups, grabbed her backpack and bounded through the front door of the diner. She was most of the way to a vacant stool by the cash register when Trudy's voice sounded.

"Koral Walker!" This time when Trudy bustled through the kitchen door, rather than a large cooking implement, she was simply holding a battered aluminum measuring cup. "Did you get your car? Did Marvin get it fixed for you?"

"It runs better than it ever has. And I think he charged me a lot less than I actually owed. I don't think he even covered his own expenses."

"Well that would be a first. It don't hurt him to do something nice for my friend."

It gave Koral a warm, good feeling to be called her friend. She smiled and said, "I brought you something."

Taking the rumpled paper bag out of her backpack, she produced the two romance novels. Delight instantly spread across Trudy's face and she reached over the counter, looping her arms around Koral's shoulders and hugging her awkwardly.

"I hope you like these. It's the least I could after all you did for me yesterday."

"Honey, I was so glad to have you stay with us. You have no idea."

"And I got a couple little treats for Jaz and Sage." She showed Trudy the candy she bought for the girls. "I hope it's okay that I got them sweets."

"I hope it's okay if they share with their momma." She tapped the measuring cup on the counter. "How about some lunch?"

Koral glanced around the inside of the diner. "I can't help but notice the skinny policeman isn't here."

"Oh Skyler, the sheriff's deputy? Why you looking for him?"

"Well, Trudy, there was an incident this morning. Skyler stopped us at his speed trap."

"I can't imagine that. Everybody knows about that trap."

"Oh, we weren't speeding. Skyler stopped us just to stop us."

"Um hmm. In other words, he was trying to impress you by showing up Four."

Koral shrugged and nodded.

"So what happened?"

"Well, to make a long story short, Four handcuffed him and left him in the back of his own police car."

"He just left him there?"

"He got on Skyler's radio and called the sheriff's office. He told them to come rescue Skyler."

Trudy nodded slowly. "Well, that's why we haven't seen the deputy today. I can't imagine how embarrassed he must be." Her head cocked slightly to one side. "How did you handle all that? Get scared?"

"Right when it was happening. I'm still a little worried about what might happen to Four. I think he was bothered on my account at first, but coming back up the mountain, he didn't seem to be worried about it at all."

"Coming back up the mountain? You rode back up here with Four? What happened to that boyfriend of yours who was supposed to bring you to your car?"

Koral stared at Trudy, deciding how to explain. "Well, he's not my boyfriend … not anymore."

"Not anymore? As in, you ditched him like a used rubber?"

She laughed. "Yeah, we did break up."

"As in, you broke it off?"

"Well, yeah."

"'Cause you're hot for Four Truett?"

Koral leaned forward, her voice low. "Can you tell?"

One eyebrow arched. "Oh honey, you're dripping with it."

"What am I going to do, Trudy? It's spring break. I'm won't get to see him for ten days."

"Says who? Sit your skinny behind on that stool and give me five minutes." She turned abruptly and disappeared into the kitchen.

Koral eased down onto the seat beside her and set her backpack on the floor. Suddenly she felt completely conspicuous. It was the first time she had been alone in the dining room and she wondered if all the customers were staring at her. She decided not to look over her shoulders to see and kept her own eyes fixed on the swinging kitchen door.

Within a couple minutes, the painfully thin waitress emerged and set a chipboard drink holder containing two large Styrofoam cups before her.

"Root beer floats," she said and turned back through the door.

Koral sat staring at the drinks. Surely Trudy was coming back with food as well—perhaps with instructions?

The door burst open again. Trudy set a white paper bag in front of her.

"Two double cheeseburgers. Two orders of fries with napkins and ketchup." She rested the backs of her hands on her aproned hips. "The way to a Truett man's heart is through his belly. So this will get you there. After that, honey, you're on your own."

She reached out for the food hesitantly. "You mean I should just take this over to his house right now?"

"That's the general idea. While it's still hot, like you. You know how to get there?"

"Oh yeah. He showed me the road yesterday."

"Um hmm. On top of that sack wrapped in tin foil is a big, well-done hamburger patty. That's for Matilda ... to make her your friend."

"Who's—oh, his dog."

"Right. Roscoe's litter mate. Near to as big and ugly as he is."

"How much is all this?"

"Don't worry about it. I put it on Marvin's tab. He got paid today."

She laughed. "I don't know how I can ever thank you for all you've done, Trudy."

"That's easy. Just come back and tell me what happens. Not all romance is in books, you know."

"Well, don't get your hopes up. I don't know that he's all that interested."

"You don't, maybe. I do. Your job is to not chicken out when it comes to pushing and shoving. Then come tell me everything. Now git." Instead of going into the kitchen, she stood looking at Koral.

"Okay then." She stooped and picked up her backpack and looped both arms through it. Scooping up the drink tray and sack, she turned and headed for the front door of the diner, somewhat relieved that almost none of the customers were watching her—though thinking at the same time she didn't care if they did.

It was no small thrill that gripped her as she set the drinks carefully in the floorboard of her car and the paper sack in the passenger's seat and tossed her book bag unceremoniously into the back. It dawned on her why she felt so powerful as she pulled off Trudy's lot headed for Four's piece of the mountain: she had a real reason to go to him. She was bringing him lunch, her way of saying "thank you" since he wouldn't let her pay him.

The anticipation she felt made it incredibly difficult to sit still as she drove. She wanted to speed. Something wild and joyous was bubbling from deep within her through her chest and arms and neck, making her wonder if she were flushed.

"I don't care. ... I really don't."

Suddenly she came to the little turn-off that led higher up the mountain to Four's house. The small apron of asphalt alongside the road was inconspicuous apart from the large tin mailbox with black lettering: "TRUETT."

"Here I come, muscle boy."

The narrow lane rose up the mountainside, bore to the right, and ran parallel to the road from which she had turned. Glancing out the passenger's window, she could see the highway through the trees a hundred feet below her. The view was breathtaking for those fleeting seconds when she took her eyes off the crowned one-lane road. It occurred to her that there might be turns and divergent paths and she wondered if she would be able to find Four's house. Surely Trudy would have told her if there were more than one possible route, if she might become lost.

After three-quarters of a mile, the grade of the road slackened and the asphalt widened slightly. She breathed a bit more deeply in relief. Next came a wooden bridge that spanned a broad, swiftly-flowing creek. She smiled.

"Caddo Creek ... how pretty."

Koral saw the house then, above the road to her left, set back 100 yards, level against the steep incline of the mountain behind it. It was a beautiful wooden A-frame, dark maple siding framing large plate-glass windows. The front porch was actually a covered deck with a swing and rocking chairs facing the road.

"I wonder who comes and rocks with him?" she asked herself.

And lying on the porch in front of the door was a massive dog, only slightly smaller than Roscoe and bearing almost identical coloring and conformation. As she pulled toward the house, the great dog lifted its head enough to look at her car. When she stopped, the dog rolled onto its legs, staring, but offering no noise or movement. Koral opened the door and stepped out, setting the white paper sack on top of her roof. At once the dog craned its neck, and when Koral pulled the wrapped hamburger patty from the bag, Matilda rose and started down the steps toward her.

"Looks like you're familiar with Trudy's cooking, too," she murmured. Then she called the dog. "Come on, Matilda. Come on, girl."

The dog loped to her without hesitation, sniffing the bag and licking at the aluminum foil as she tried to unwrap it. Koral scarcely got the patty exposed before the dog had grabbed it with her teeth and gobbled it and looked back up to her expectantly.

"That's really all I brought for you, girl. Hope you don't eat me and my lunch, too."

Koral heard the front door open. She looked up to see Four standing on the porch—his shirttail pulled out, barefoot, holding a microbiology textbook in his free hand. They stared at each other. Finally she decided to be the one to speak.

"Want some lunch?"

His face lightened. "That sack looks like it came from Trudy's."

"Cheeseburgers, fries and root beer floats."

"Works for me." He held open the front door. "Want to sit up to the kitchen table?"

"Is it okay just to sit out here in the rockers?"

"Sure." He pulled two close together and straightened them to face the road. "Stay down there, Matilda. You had your treat. Why don't you go catch me a rabbit?"

The dog ambled toward the side of the house as if on command. As she carried the food up the steps, Koral watched the dog.

"Does she understand you?"

"I don't think so. She hasn't yet brought me a single bunny." He sat in one of the rockers and accepted a burger from Koral. "This is awful nice of you."

"Well, you wouldn't let me pay you. And, having ridden in your car, I don't think it's going to break down anytime soon, much as I do want my picture made."

Sitting down in the rocker, she faced away from the house for the first time and gasped at the view. Cascading below her was the panorama of the road, beneath which was the mountain stream and a tumble of ridges, each crowned with a copse of trees in different stages of blossom and foliage.

"God! What a view."

"You're right. God does live here … though further up the mountain, I'm told."

She sat transfixed, gazing from one edge of the horizon to the other. "Do you ever get tired of this?"

"Real beauty never gets old." He glanced at her. "That's how I knew you broke it off, not him."

She turned to Four. "What?"

"I asked if you had some fries in that bag."

"Oh yeah. And here's your float." She gazed over either shoulder at the wood and glass structure. "How long have you lived here?"

"I've lived in this house all my life. My dad built it when he came back from Vietnam. Further up the road about a mile is where the big house was. My great-granddad built it. My dad and his kid brother Elvis and my Aunt Eleanor grew up there. It burned when I was just a kid. Lightning strike."

"So are you the only one in your family who lives here now?"

He took a big drink of his float. "For the time being. 'Til my dad gets out of jail. I'm hoping he moves back up here."

"Why wouldn't he? It's his mountain, isn't it?"

"Technically it's mine. That was part of his plea deal. He had to surrender ownership of the property where he had been growing dope. Since I had no record and was next of kin, he could deed it to me."

"What happened to the rest of your family?"

He paused to wipe his mouth with a napkin. "My grandparents died in a head-on car wreck when I was about six. It was over near Siloam Springs. They were hit by a drunk driver, which I guess is sort of ironic, although Dad always said it wasn't one of my grandpa's customers.

"Aunt Eleanor, the baby of the family, married, moved away from the mountain, and was widowed. She has a story worth hearing. Then there is my Uncle Elvis. He's in the wind."

She stared at him uncertainly. "I'm kind of afraid to ask what that means."

Four laughed. "It means my uncle is a fugitive from justice and nobody knows where he is. And even those of us who do know where he is aren't going to admit to knowing for another three-and-a-half-years."

"Why not?"

"'Cause the statute of limitations isn't over 'til then. Elvis wasn't in the famous shoot-out, but he had been in business with Dad. He took off when Dad got arrested, and he ain't coming back until the time expires when they can charge him.

"Elvis and his wife Teeny got divorced after their two sons, my cousins Marvin and Wesley, graduated from high school and moved out. Teeny lives over in Van Buren. Wesley is married and works as a city mechanic for North Little Rock."

"Well, you didn't say anything about your mom. Is she still living?"

He wadded his hamburger wrapper and dropped it in the sack. "Mom is living and living it up. Seems, when I was a kid, a preacher was serving at a little church down the mountain. He heard about the Truetts and their profligate ways and decided to convert my mom." He smiled at her. "Turns out she converted him. They ran off together. Now they live in Shreveport. I get a card from her at Christmas."

Koral finished her float and slipped the empty cup into the white bag. "You certainly have an interesting family, Four Truett."

"I guess that's a nice way to put it." He dropped his trash in the bag. "Thanks for bringing lunch."

"Well, I was in the neighborhood." She was determined not to let him know how anxious she felt. "As long as I'm here, maybe you could show me your orchard. I can tell you what you're doing wrong."

Koral could tell her words surprised him. For an instant he was speechless. A broad smile broke across his face.

"Hard to turn down an offer like that from you, professor. The question is, which orchard do you want to see? If you don't mind climbing 1500 feet, I have some apples in a south-facing meadow. Then five miles around on the west side I have pecans and hickories and a few walnuts maybe."

Koral gave him an impatient look. "You have a road up to these places surely. Even you are smart enough not to plant trees where you can't get to them."

"There are roads and I have an old truck I drive up to all my orchards, but I only use the truck when I'm actually working on the trees. Giving guided tours to flatland grad students isn't really work in my book so, if you want to see 'em, you have to walk." He leaned back in his rocker. "Tell you what, Miss Walker, the closest stand of bearing trees I got is my peach orchard. It's about a quarter mile from here. Maybe even a city girl like you can make it that far."

She crumpled the trash bag with an expression of disdain. "I'm ready when you are, muscle boy."

He whistled sharply, just put his tongue to the roof of his mouth and blew a shrill note. It surprised her and she jumped. By the time she had drawn a deep breath to calm herself, the dog trotted back into view, staring up at them from the driveway.

"Stay, 'Tilda." He opened the front door and retrieved a worn pair of sneakers and then motioned toward the steps. "Shall we?"

After he tugged on his shoes, they walked down the steps and around the side of his house. It was larger than it had seemed to Koral at first glance. The sharply rising mountain behind it prevented her from recognizing how long it was. And beneath the overhanging eaves were more of the large plate-glass windows. She wondered if it were intrusive of her to gaze inside at the furnishings and accessories of Four's life.

The grade of the earth rose steeply as they walked along parallel to the road below them. Song birds trilled and soared in the still air. Koral would have gazed about her at the immense vistas had the ground been even and dependable.

"So I have a question for you."

She glanced at him. "Yeah?"

"Why do you call me muscle boy?"

"... I don't know. Do you want me to stop?"

"No. I was just curious."

"Well, I have a question for you."

"Okay."

"Why do you hardly ever call me Koral?"

"Hmm. Guess I don't feel like I know you that well. It's nothing personal. It's the way I was raised. I know I'm pretty much poor white trash, but I was raised to be respectful."

Koral set her jaw. "First, I don't think you or any of your family are poor white trash. You are different from my family, but not worse. Just very different. You in particular are a decorated war hero. I know you got wounded saving the lives of other Marines. That makes you pretty special in my mind. But, on the other hand, if you were raised to be so respectful, why do you constantly tease me?"

"Tease you?"

"Don't act so innocent. You know what I'm talking about. You give me a bad time about being a flatlander and a grad student and being naive. And I'm not, you know. I'm really a lot more worldly than you're giving me credit for."

He chuckled. "Well, you're two different people to me, Koral Walker. On the one hand, you're the ideal woman. You're very bright and—and lots of other things. You aren't afraid of life. You've traveled around. You've got a real career ahead of you. You can field strip an M-14 rifle. What guy could ask for more? But then I do think you are kind of innocent and sheltered and not ready for the real world."

"Do tell?"

"Oh yeah. I did an internet search last night. I entered 'typical foolishly idealistic graduate student' and your picture popped right up."

"Oh!" She grimaced. "You're such a shit. I think I've just figured out the real reason you don't have a girl. And by the way, I did a search for 'conceited backward mountain muscle boy' and guess whose bio came up?"

He stopped. "Well, here we are."

Koral had been so intent on the conversation and the ground

before her that she had not seen the cloistered meadow as they approached it. She stopped to take in the site. The steep mountainside provided sheltering walls on two sides for the orchard, dozens and dozens of short, spayed trees just breaking forth into bloom.

"It's four acres," he said. "The cliffs hold back the north and west wind. It's the only place on the mountain I'd try to grow peaches. They're kind of delicate. And this is the best time to see them. In a few days the blooms will be completely open and the aviaries would carry you away."

She stood looking in silence at cleverly spaced ranks of trees. And Four watched her.

"Aren't you going to tell me?" he asked.

"Tell you what?"

"What I've done wrong."

She sighed. "Well, you're lucky."

"Lucky? Why's that?"

"Lucky a late frost hasn't taken out every bud."

"Actually we did have a couple late frosts. I used misters to save the blossoms."

"Misters?"

"What a shock. There's something about horticulture you don't know? If you use mist to put some humidity in the air and if it doesn't get too cold, the blooms are protected from the frost to a degree, and they don't die."

"What's that?"

"What's what?"

"Over there just past the dirt road. Is that a greenhouse?"

"Yep. That's where I do my grafting and take care of the saplings. Want to see?"

It was a low-ceilinged glass building, narrow across the front and long to the back, with pale green filament covering the copious windows. Moisture beaded on the glass, making it difficult to see inside from the bright meadow.

Koral followed him in, standing just inside the door and letting her eyes adjust. Five long rows of tables stretched from the front of the building to the back, covered with small trees, vines and sprouts sitting in buckets and clay pots.

"Oh, my god," she said softly. She shook her head. "How do you have time for this? How do you plant all these orchards and prune and harvest and grow all this stuff?"

He shrugged. "Easy. I don't have a life. This is my life."

Koral glanced at a writing desk and sofa just inside the door along the glass wall. "You study up here?"

Four put his hands on his hips. "I stay out here some nights. It helps me with my memories."

"You have memory loss?"

"Ha. I wish …. No, some nights I can't sleep because of the memories I can't get out of my head, like the melody to a song you don't really like, but you can't quit humming. So I tell 'Tilda to keep an eye on the house, and I walk up here and sit on the couch facing the orchard. When your eyes get accustomed to the dark, you can see all kinds of critters moving through the trees. Deer. Possums. Coons. Rabbits. Watching for them gets my mind off my memories. The next thing you know, I'm waking up. It's morning."

Koral drew a deep breath. The feeling that enveloped her earlier in the shower slipped over her again.

"You bring lots of girls up here, Four Truett, to show them your secret greenhouse?"

"… No, actually. I guess you're the first person I brought up here since I built it."

"Why'd you bring me?" She turned toward him completely.

"Well, now that you mention it, you're the only person I know who would really appreciate it."

"Well, I do. I think it's amazing."

He nodded slowly. "I think you're amazing."

She felt as if she were trembling. She wanted to reach out and put her arms around him—or, even more, for him to put his arms around her.

"Amazing good or amazing bad?"

His head tilted slightly to one side, he stared at her with an expression of curiosity. "You have no idea, do you, of how appealing and marvelous you are? You have no idea of the power you have over—over guys."

"… Over you?"

He nodded. "I'm a guy."

Koral was transfixed by the color of his eyes, sea blue with flecks of gold. She watched as her hand slowly moved to his face and caressed his firm, pliant cheek.

"Are you going to kiss me, Four Truett, or just leave me standing here like an idiot?"

Chapter 5

Although Four Truett's bedroom window faced east, the light of emerging dawn did not shine directly in Koral's eyes. The eaves of the A-frame house extended down far enough to screen out the sun as it crested the horizon, but not so far that she couldn't see the still, variegated forest through which the dappled sunlight crept, creating tall, thin, slowly-moving shadows.

The tranquility of the woods outside the window was matched by the serenity of the room where she lay naked on her side—covered with clean sheets and an old, hand-stitched quilt—gazing through the plate glass. The only sound was the regular breathing of the man lying on his back, his shoulder gently pressed against the space between her shoulder blades.

Instead of asking herself how she felt, she realized she was wondering how she should feel. Shouldn't she feel guilty, remorseful for the way she had pursued and forced herself on this—well, he wasn't a boy exactly? Though when he let down his guard, so much about him was boyish.

She closed her eyes, remembering the desperate clinging of their twined limbs. Should she feel wanton? Should she feel perverse, not merely for their multiple couplings, but as well for the unabashed hunger of their bodies for each other and the way they continued until they were sated?

Four made the slightest moaning sound, as if overhearing her internal dialogue and commenting on it. She looked over her shoulder at him. Whatever she should be feeling, she felt no regret. Should she regret feeling no regret?

There was some embarrassment she felt. It had to do with the way she had talked continually the first time they made love, something that was absurdly unlike her—or at the very least, completely unique, so she could not say she would never do it again, only that she had never done it before.

"I don't do this," she had said as he lowered her onto her back on the old sofa in the greenhouse. "I mean, of course, I've done this. I mean I'm never this …"

"…What?" He had asked when she could not find the words.

She was distracted at that instant by the delightful texture of his hands sliding up the small of her back, beneath her bra strap and the feel of suddenly being liberated from it, of waiting to feel his fingers on her breasts.

"Forward. I'm not … uh … really I'm not forward. I'm not like this."

"Like what?" His voice was soft. Heavy. Like the sound of a bass guitar played slowly and alone. "You mean you really don't feel like this? …. You don't taste like this? …. Your nipples don't stand up like this?"

"Ah … I mean, when I opened up your shirt like that. Even before … when I pressed up against you … um … when we were first kissing …"

Even as he lifted her neck upward and kissed her throat and the underside of her chin and let his bare chest down onto hers, she was remembering how it was when they were standing and first embraced. Remembering how she was the one who pulled their bodies tightly together and how it seemed to surprise him. And how she forced her mouth against his and sucked his tongue between her lips. Remembering how she became aware of the growing tumescence as his member, parallel to the ground, grew hard between them and shifted until it was nearly perpendicular; and she in response had placed her hand on his behind and pressed them together even more firmly.

And as she remembered, she became aware that he had lifted himself off her and rolled to one side, looking at her with amazement, desire and caution. Gently he placed his hand on her stomach. They looked at it together. She realized he was waiting … waiting for her assent.

Her voice had a ragged quality, as if she were trying to catch her breath. "You can either make love to me right now, or I can just lie here and explode."

He studied her face. "All over my plants?"

"It's up to you, muscle boy. What better way for a botanist to die?"

"Well—" He kissed one breast, his tongue coarse against the

helplessly taut nipple. "—really, you should live before you die."

She watched her hand as it reached down, with a certainty belying the anxiety she felt, and firmly unlatched his belt and undid the top button of his jeans. And he slowly, as if savoring, unfastened her jeans and loosened them and began to kiss from her belly button gradually down to the top of her pubis, sliding her panties down with his tongue as he progressed.

At that her back arched and her head rolled back, her eyes closed, and she began to speak. "Is this really happening? Are we really ... doing this? It doesn't seem possible that it's real."

"Let me know if you figure it out, Miss Walker."

" ... Can you call me Koral? .... Can you say, 'Koral, how does it feel ... when I touch you ... there. Koral, why did you fall for me so hard? Koral ... why do you make me so hard? Why ... are you so wet, Koral'?"

He kissed her on the mouth ... a sweet, long kiss. A kiss of confession, conceding at last without words the affection he felt for her. A kiss that poured forth from him and drew forth from her an achingly beautiful mutuality, a shared intimacy beyond verbal expression ... though afterwards she drew a quivering breath and began to talk again.

"It's too soon to say 'I love you,' isn't it? If I ... Oh, Four! .... Mmm ... If I say I love you ... don't think it's just because ... we're making love .... I mean, we are, but ... that's not why I love you .... Well, partly, I mean .... Just like that .... Oh my god ... Just like that ... right there. Oh ... That's good, too .... I'm stupid, aren't I ... for telling you I love you? Oh ... I can't take it back, though. Really ... Oh ... I don't want ... to. Oh, oh ... Oh-oh. I should tell you ... I'm not easily ... not easily ... Oh-oh!"

"Orgasmic? You're not easily ... orgasmic?"

" ... No. Never."

" ... So what was that then? You were faking that sound?"

"Mmm. No ... Was that disgusting? Ohhhh ...?"

"Actually, it's erotic as hell ... arousing .... Just like that one was .... As if ... I needed to be aroused .... Oh. Oh."

"Oh god. I can't help myself .... I have ... noises coming out of me ... everywhere. I can't stop ... talking. Ohhh. Ohhh, Four ... Don't ... make ... me ... come ... again."

Yet she did, as loud and uncontrollable as the ones that came before. And her limbs lost all purchase, her arms flowing outward onto the roughly upholstered couch, her legs flaccidly riding on the hips of the boy no longer pounding but rhythmically pressing his crotch against hers. Then he, too, seemed to falter and droop slowly until the length of them sandwiched. She could feel his heart pounding through her right breast. Still another sensation experienced for the first time.

She lifted her hand to his face, as she had when they first embraced, and spoke. "Oh my god, Four …. Oh my god."

And he, studying her closely despite his ragged breathing, replied. "Is that all you have to say?"

They laughed. Languorously she looped her arms around his neck and kissed him.

"I said way too much …. I must confess, however, I failed in my actual intent."

"Do tell?"

"Yes. I had no intention of making love to you."

"Oh?"

"I just wanted to get you naked so I could see your leg. And, you know, somehow I didn't get even a glimpse."

He nodded, considering. "Well, what if we try again? Soon as I catch my breath. Then maybe you can get a look."

So they had. Once again in the greenhouse and twice in Four's bed, once before and once after supper. Oddly she had been little concerned about the pitted thigh and scarred calf, apart from realizing he didn't have terribly "bad leg," but also realizing she couldn't tell Jaz she had seen it.

And that memory, as she lay on her side—completely bare beneath the crisp sheets, gazing out his window at the awakening morning—made her smile.

How should she feel? She did not know. What she did feel was an inner stillness. It was serenity. And neither was she anxious concerning what this day would bring.

The touch of his fingertips along the side of her neck surprised her. She didn't realize he was awake. Koral rolled onto her back and found him gazing back at her.

He cleared his throat. "Hi."

"Hi. I want to tell you something."

"What?"

She turned onto her side to face him. "I'm not easy."

He gave her the mischievous, boyish smile she had begun to see more and more throughout the previous evening. "Well, I tell you. Maybe you're right. The first three or four times were pretty easy. After that, it kind of got to be work."

Her jaw dropped. "We did not make love five times yesterday."

"Twice in front of my saplings. Then once for an appetizer. And once for dessert. And don't forget what happened when you weren't sure where the bathroom was in the dark."

"That was after midnight," she protested. "That was today. That wasn't yesterday."

"Hmm. A natural mistake on my part. And, to be honest, it was actually a lot more pleasure than work."

"I just want to say—" She rolled onto her back again. "This sort of thing doesn't happen to me."

"Yeah. You were saying something like that in the greenhouse while you were taking off my pants. Why is it so important for you to tell me that?"

"It just is. I just want you to know I don't—well, I never had—done anything remotely like that before. And I think—you know—in the heat of the moment—"

"It wasn't just hot. It was wet."

"Yeah. I know. As I was trying to say, I might have been swept away in the moment, told you I loved you—a couple times."

"Four times. But who's counting."

"Well, however many. I'm just saying that all this isn't like me."

" … So you're saying you really don't love me."

"No. No, I'm not saying anything about love. I'm saying I hope you don't hold against me what I said and did."

" … I kind of liked everything you said and did."

"Oh, Four." She kissed him, her hands on either side of his face. "I'm just trying to say I'm not a floozy. I'm really not a girl who goes to bed with a guy she's only known for two days."

He remained silent for so long, looking into her eyes, that she began to fear she had somehow said something terrible, something that would drive him away.

"Would it help," he asked slowly, "if I told you I had known you for longer than two days?"

" … What?"

76

"What if I said I had known you since the middle of January, from the first day of class, when you came in wearing that crazy purple stole with the matching gloves and the dark green parka, looking like a little kid? And that pencil-neck boyfriend of yours hovered around you so close, so as to leave no doubt you belonged to him. And about the time you sat down, you turned around to speak to someone you knew, and I saw the blue fire dancing in your eyes. *Schwarz hair, blau augen.* A German girl with perfect features and full of such joy .... You set the hook in me deep that first day, Koral.

"So each time class met, I watched for you. I got there early and waited for you and grad boy to show up. You made me crazy because you always came in at the last minute, so I never got to hear much of your voice. And when I did, it was like listening to a happy little girl .... And I could tell you had no idea—no idea—how special you are."

Even though she had started to cry, her mouth open in silent astonishment, he continued. "I loved to listen to you answer questions. I loved the way Dr. Hanley would pick the hardest, most obscure part of the chapter we were studying to try to trip you up. And you knew your stuff. And you teased him in your ... little girl, feminine way."

He used the sheet to wipe her eyes and nose. "I never thought we would ever speak .... And I made myself okay with that. There are all kind of things in life we want and we aren't going to experience. You were one of those unfulfilled dreams for me.

"Then the day before yesterday this car started breaking down in front of me as I was driving up the mountain. At first all I could see at the distance was the back of the driver's head. I thought, 'What wishful thinking. That looks just like Miss Walker.' But about the time you pulled over, I was close enough to see your eyes in your rearview mirror. I thought, 'Oh my god. It is her. What am I going to do?' So I decided to be all business. I decided to show no sign of how I felt about you."

She shook her head. "Why, Four? Why did you make me do all the work? Why didn't you let me know some way that you cared for me?"

"'Cause I'm damaged goods, Koral. I'm not good enough for you. I don't know a better way to say it .... Probably I wasn't worthy of you before I got blown up. But now—for sure—I'm just fucking crazy .... Honest. Sometimes I don't know what I'm going to do."

"Like, are you violent?"

"No. You mean, would I hurt somebody? No. At least I don't think so. I mean, you saw me with Skyler. I think those situations, where there's possible danger, are actually the safest for me. I know what to do and how to do it."

" ... Well, what then? Why do you think you're so crazy?"

Four rolled onto his back. "It's nights mostly, Koral. I get afraid to sleep sometimes. I don't know if I'm dreaming or not. Sometimes I go two or three days without sleeping."

"Well, have you been to the VA—"

"Christ, don't get me started on those jokers .... I think I've done an awful thing, Koral. I've let us get close—not just physically, but emotionally. I was weak to let it happen. Now I can't think how to undo it." He reached out and brushed her cheek with the tips of his fingers. "You were so near to me, though. And you wanted me as much as I wanted you." He shook his head. "I just couldn't resist."

She propped her head in hand, her elbow on the bed. "...So you're saying you want me out of your life?"

"Of course not. You're the most spectacular thing that ever happened to me. I'd have to be crazy to want you out of my life .... Hmm. I'm crazy, but if I want you in my life, I'm not crazy. Maybe I'm not as crazy as I thought."

"Well." Her voice was coy, girlish. "In my experience, when people say 'I'd have to be crazy' to do something, they really mean what they are considering is illogical ... not insane. Like, 'I'd have to be crazy to gamble with my rent money at the casino,' really means, 'It would be so foolish to risk losing my rent'." She ran her free hand down his throat and onto his chest. "So actually you can love me and want me in your life and still be as crazy as you want."

Slowly a wry smile spread across his face. "You're so damn cool. Maybe you can help me figure out what gross, disgusting thing it would take to make you fly back down the mountain and forget all about Four Truett and Caddo Creek."

"So your plan is to disgust me so that I never want anything to do with you again? Is that right?"

"Pretty much. At first I thought just having to deal with my cousin would do the trick. But no. Speaking of which—" He sat halfway up, looking at the clock on the nightstand. "—Marvin is going to be here in about ninety minutes to take me and my kayak up the mountain."

"Oh! To float down the creek? I want to go."

Once again he stared at her silently. And once again she wondered why her words had affected him so.

"Is it a two-man?" she asked.

"Well, yes. I have one that is."

"I'm not helpless on the water. I can paddle a canoe, which I think is a lot harder than a kayak."

".... I don't know what I'm going to find up on the mountain, Koral. I'm not fooling when I say it could be really, really dangerous."

"Dangerous? There's something more dangerous on this mountain than you? I'd have to see that to believe it."

His voice was not harsh, but somehow very serious. "And you can't talk to anybody about what you see on the mountain. Are you still game?"

"Sure. Sounds mysterious."

"All right then. We can take a shower and I'll fix us breakfast. But there is one situation I might need some assistance with before we get started."

"What's that?"

He lifted the sheets gradually until she could see his rock-hard erection.

"Oh my. That looks almost painful. I think I can help relieve it, though. In the future when you develop a condition like this, make sure you bring it to my attention."

Standing inside the front door, Koral could see Marvin as he rolled up in his creaky pickup, but he could not see her. She grinned at the sight of him staring at her Toyota, parked along the gravel drive. She opened the door and stepped out, standing demurely, her hands on the rail and a coy smile on her face.

"Hello, Miss Walker," he said, easing out the door. "Something wrong with your car? You couldn't make it down the mountain?"

"Oh, not at all, Marvin. It runs like a top. How are you this morning?"

"Too soon to tell," he replied, seeming still perplexed by why she and her car were at Four's home.

"And your lovely wife, Trudy? How is she? And your darling girls?"

"This is Trudy's Saturday off. Her cousin Mitchell is cooking at the diner today." He stretched. "His specialty is pancakes. Trudy and the girls slept in. They were just getting up when I left."

"Oh. I hope you had breakfast," she said brightly. "Four fixed us omelets."

Marvin nodded. "With hot sauce, I hope. He really knows how to make them."

That was the instant Four appeared from the side of the house carrying a sky-blue kayak. He was wearing a backpack and—Koral thought—an odd expression, like those she had seen on the faces of soldiers loading onto planes to be deployed.

Marvin approached him and spoke, his voice so soft Koral could scarcely hear him. "Hey, cousin. I was thinking this was hush-hush."

Four slid the kayak into the bed of the truck. Hands on hips, he faced Marvin and replied. "You weren't even here today, buck. And if you don't see me anytime soon, don't come looking for me."

"Jesus, Four. It's like that, but you're taking the girl?"

"Yeah, well." He put his good leg on the corroded bumper and stepped up to the bed of the truck. "Ain't the first stupid thing I've done." He turned to her. "Coming along, Miss Walker?"

She bounced down the front steps and took his outstretched hand. They sat with their backs against the cab as Marvin started up the truck. Despite her awareness of the men's ominous tone, she had a feeling of lightness she could not dissuade. She wondered if Four thought she looked stupid, what with the way she sat looking at him with a huge smile as his cousin pulled back onto the one-lane road and drove further up the mountain. Whatever he might have been thinking, he did not reveal. He did, however, reach out and take her hand in his after a time and return her smile.

Koral was not sure how long they rode up the mountain, first on the blacktop and then abruptly turning off of it and onto a rutted dirt path. The ride alternated between pure, childlike joy and moments of sharp pain when one wheel or another dropped into a hole unseen beneath the vegetation covering the path. Eventually Marvin slowed and stopped. And Koral immediately heard the gurgling, rushing sound of a stream.

Before the truck had completely ceased moving, Four had pulled himself to his feet and slung his pack over one shoulder. He helped Koral to her feet and hopped to the ground. Together with Marvin he slid the kayak off the bed of the truck.

As she stepped onto the bumper and down into the knee-high grass, Koral studied the narrow stream. Birch and gum saplings grew alongside the water. Despite its noisy ripples, the creek had a calming impact on her. The water, she knew, would be remarkably cold.

It dawned on her that the men were speaking to each other again, intentionally keeping their voices low. Marvin slapped his cousin on the shoulder and pulled himself back into the cab of the truck. Four watched as the pickup pulled around them and disappeared back down the mountain road. Then, hands on hips again, he turned to her.

"What's in the backpack?" she asked. "Lunch?"

"Not exactly."

"So what's the big mystery about a float trip?"

He unzipped the back pouch of the bag, reaching deep within. "Remember our little conversation? How I said this could be dangerous?"

" … Yeah?"

"I wasn't joking." He produced a pistol in a belted holster. "You recognize this, Miss Side-Arms-Expert?" He held it out to her.

"Looks like a medium-caliber Smith and Wesson revolver." She took it and unlatched the leather hammer guard. "Like maybe a .38 Special. And it's loaded with hollow nipple rounds."

"Right. And there are two speed loaders on the belt. Why don't you go ahead and put that on?" he said, digging into the backpack once again.

Wordlessly fastening the belt around her waist, she watched as he produced a semi-automatic pistol and began to strap it on himself.

"And that," she said, "is an awesome nine-millimeter Browning Repeater. Do you mind me asking why we're toting such high-powered, high-class hardware?"

"I let you come along with me today because you can handle these, Koral. I hope we don't need them—and probably we won't."

"Well, just as a heads up, can you tell me what exactly will we be shooting at? Do you have mountain lions up here?"

"Never seen any cougars or panthers," he said. He pushed the kayak until its nose was in the water and handed her one of the tandem paddles. "I've been told they aren't totally extinct in the Ozarks, though. There are bears, however. There are coyotes."

"Moccasins?"

"Usually not at this high of an elevation." He motioned for her to climb into the front bucket. "This water is a little cold and swift for them. Ready?"

They pushed away from the bank into the center of the creek. The urgent rush of the water against the kayak ceased. For an instant it seemed there was no motion at all. Caught in the flow of the current, they floated slowly in the mountain stream. Their pace was gradual enough that she could observe and name each species of tree crowding the water's edge: cottonwood, willow, hackberry, sycamore.

"It's beautiful up here, Four. And peaceful."

"It is, isn't it? When I was a kid, I had my grandpa take me way up here on the mountain. I'd float halfway down and camp out overnight. Then I'd float the rest of the way down the next morning."

"Your family let you do that?"

"Yep."

"I take it they weren't as afraid of the bears back then as you are now."

"Ha. Well, there weren't mules on the mountain back then."

"Mules?"

"Yep. They can be the most dangerous of all."

With her back to him, she could not see his expression. His evasiveness only heightened her curiosity, which warred for her attention with the awe she felt floating in the still creek. She heard his paddle dip into the clear water but knew he did not need her help. The strong, slow current was pulling them down the stream. Four was only keeping them in the deepest part of the water.

They came to a place in the creek where the stream narrowed. Trees on both banks—mostly oaks and maples—grew over the water, providing a full canopy of graceful shade. The quiet and beauty filled her with tranquility. And there a light, sweet fragrance wafting about them, embracing them.

She turned to ask but he, in anticipation, answered before she spoke. "Honeysuckle. It's out early this spring."

"How far is it to where we're going?"

"Five miles from where we started to the low water bridge by my house … just a mile to where we're stopping first, though."

"Where are we stopping first?"

" … You remember me telling you I had an apple orchard up high on the mountain?"

His voice had a different quality to it. She had heard it before, though—the previous day when he realized Skyler was behind them in his deputy's car, the lights flashing.

"Yeah?"

"We're going through the back door."

"Okay …. What's the back door of an orchard?"

" … Well, if the north-facing part facing the road is the front door, then the south-facing side is the back door."

"And the creek runs beside it?"

"Pretty close, about a quarter mile through heavy brush."

"All right. I'm with you," she said. She fought the urge to crane her neck and look at him. "So why are you coming at your orchard from the back way instead of from the road? And what kind of trouble makes you feel the need to be armed—and not with shotguns or rifles, but pistols?"

He seemed to be thinking the question over. "Well, you're going to find out soon enough. I heard a rumor that other people have been planting things on my mountain."

"How can that be? The only road in goes right by your house."

"Two possible ways. First, there are three days a week I'm not on Caddo Creek. You could have a hundred people planting and harvesting and I'd never know it. Second, there's a landing strip on the far side at the top. Planes can come and go and I wouldn't hear them."

"So," she asked, "if people are on your mountain, are you going to chase them off?"

He made a low, chuckling sound. "Well, all I'm doing right now is verifying. I learned in the Marines that there's a difference sometimes between what you hear and what's true."

She wished again she could see his face and try at least to cut through the mystery. "Do you think they'll attack you if you try to kick them off?"

"Maybe …. You're not afraid, are you?"

"Well, no … Not really."

He laughed. "Yeah, you are. I can tell it in your voice." He paused as he corrected the direction of the kayak once again. "Look,

Koral, we're almost there .... I need you to do just what I tell you. From this point on, everything is a whisper. When we port the boat, I want you to scoot that holster around so the piece is on your back hip—not too far for you to reach, but so it can't be seen from the front. I want you to walk right behind me, your steps in my steps. Roger on all this?"

Koral nodded, the feeling of apprehension welling within her.

Somehow Four managed to beach the kayak beside a birch tree, running it far enough onto the bank that neither had to step into the water to get out. He turned it around to face the creek and placed the paddles along the edges. He was preparing, she recognized, for a swift exit from the "back door".

Her father told her of infantry who were trained to walk so quietly that those walking before and behind them could not hear their steps. The memory of his words came back to her as she followed in Four's absolutely silent footsteps. They moved through the heavy brush with caution and surprising swiftness.

She wasn't sure how far they had traveled—several hundred meters, it seemed—when he stopped abruptly. He produced a double-edged combat knife and knelt to the forest floor. His movements were strangely artistic, casual yet focused and exact, as he swept the blade along, clearing foliage from the path before them. At a point he paused and put the blade against the dirt directly before them, enabling Koral to see what he was working on.

She caught her breath, struggling to remain silent at the sight of an anti-personnel mine. It was, she knew, capable of killing or dismembering both of them. A trip wire ran from either side of the mine. Four deftly removed the lines and disengaged the mechanism. Hacking at the ground, he exposed and examined the edges of the mine, then lifted it in his hand and held it before them. He put an index finger against his lips and nodded down the path.

Another fifty meters down the trail, Four stopped again. He climbed through the heavy undergrowth parallel to the path and stopped at a little bluff overlooking a swale. The tiny valley beneath them seemed hidden in shadows. Koral realized at once that a net of some kind was stretched over the ground a dozen feet in the air; and she realized as well that vividly green bushes were growing in rows across the length and breadth of the swale, covering at least two acres of ground.

She whispered in Four's ear so softly she could not hear her own words. "What is it?"

He turned to her and spoke aloud. "How can you not recognize marijuana? Time to let my guests know I'm here."

Four produced the anti-personnel mine and stepped back onto the trail. He smiled up and waved at a crook in an ash tree. Koral suddenly saw a small video camera perched there. Four had diverted them from the trail when he saw it. Now he was holding the mine in front of the camera—pointing to it with his finger.

From 200 meters down the valley on the other side of the cannabis patch, Koral heard a man's excited exclamation: "*Ai! Ai! Ai!*"

And Four, when he heard it, smashed the camera with the handle of his knife and sheathed it.

"Yeah, I know this guy," Four said. "Just be cool and stay back by the trees. If anything happens, follow the trail back to the kayak and go straight down the creek."

"But—"

From below them, there was a thrashing sound of a man pushing his way through foliage and climbing uphill. Koral could not see him for the brush, but she could hear him easily. By the time he was within twenty meters, she could also hear his labored breathing. He paused, hidden from sight, though both Four and she stared at the foliage behind which he was concealed. The barrel of an AK47 protruded through the brush, pushing aside the branches, and a young Hispanic man in camouflage fatigues cautiously appeared. He glanced at her, then turned his gaze to Four.

"Truett. I heard you were down at the college."

"Jorge. How are you? What are you doing up here on my mountain?"

The Latino smiled broadly. "I'm just doing a little gardening, keeping my hand in, you know, until your daddy gets back." He kept the barrel of the automatic rifle pointed in Four's general direction. Ten feet separated the two men. Koral's hands hung at her sides as she contemplated how quickly she could produce the .38.

"My daddy is out of the dope-growing business," Four replied. "Permanently. I don't think you have the *caballos* to put in a stand like this yourself, Jorge. I'm guessing Mr. Deere is the man behind this."

"No." Jorge shook his head, unconvincingly. "This is just my little garden."

"I'm also guessing this isn't just a few acres. I'm betting there are eight or nine or more plots on around the mountain, maybe two dozen acres. Or more. And I can guess just where they are."

Koral's focus remained on Jorge. From the corner of her eye, she saw Four hold out the land mine—in far too cavalier a manner, she thought.

"And what about this here, amigo? You have these around all the fields, don't you? You trying to kill somebody on my mountain?"

"Oh no, Truett." He shook his head vigorously. "I just can't be everywhere, you know. I'm not trying to hurt nobody."

"It's not your style anyway, Jorge," Four said, casually disarming the mine and tossing it into the brush. "My dad sure never taught you that. It does, however, seem to me like something Hamilton Deere would do to protect his investment, leaving you here to risk your life and freedom while he's off in Hot Springs racing horses."

Jorge's eyes narrowed. The barrel of the Kalashnikov, Koral thought, moved a bit in Four's direction.

"This is my operation, I tol' you. Start to finish. And I will keel whoever gets in my way."

Four shrugged. "Well, you haven't killed me."

Jorge tilted his head. "What is it you want, Truett?"

Immediately he answered. "Half."

For the second time, Koral caught her breath, trying to show no visible response. Was it possible? Four was claiming profits from the marijuana growing on his mountain? She need not have worried about keeping silent because Jorge burst out with laughter.

"Half? Deere will never give you half. He would keel you first."

"That's just the thing. Deere don't know who to kill, does he? You think I'd come up here unarmed and face you like this if I didn't have others in the know backing me up?"

The Latino's eyes narrowed. "What if Deere says 'no'? He gives orders. He don't take them. You can't turn him in. You can't prove thees is his grass. What can you do? Try to steal the crop?"

"I'll poison the crop. And I'll do it so he doesn't know. I'm not studying ag for nothing. Deere will be selling weed that makes people sick, that kills people. Word gets around. Everybody knows this is his crop. Money and jail will be the least of his problems."

Jorge stared at Four, thinking the situation over. "I don't think he's going to jus' take my word for it that he should geev you half his cash, bro."

Four nodded. "That's why you're going to tell him to meet me on the mountain Monday night. Just him, Jorge. Not you. None of his goons. He comes alone. I come alone. Tell him, for every man he brings with him, his share gets cut in half."

For an instant Koral cut her eyes toward Four. She wanted to glimpse his expression, to gauge for herself if he truly was going to extort drug money. Just for a fleeting second she turned her glance— just her eyes—toward this man whom she realized she did not know at all. And Jorge recognized in that moment the change upon her countenance, so that he set his gaze on her. He studied her, his face etched with curiosity, trying to decide what she was to this hard mountain man who had appeared suddenly, making such harsh demands.

He nodded toward Koral and asked, "*Quien es la puta?*"

His words seemed to surprise Four. For an instant Koral thought he had not understood the question. Then a reflective look crossed his face, as if he had entirely forgotten she was with him. Four began to turn toward her, as if to see whom Jorge was asking about; and the second he did, Jorge's eyes turned with his toward Koral.

Then, with quickness that astonished her and took the drug mule completely off guard, Four snapped back toward him and forced the barrel of the rifle upward. He stepped across the larger man's body, rocking him with a hand to the throat, throwing him backward and tripping him across Four's extended foot. As Jorge hit the path, Four stripped the piece from him, righted it in his own hands and brought the muzzle alongside the Latino's left ear. He fired once into the ground and, as his adversary jumped, he fired a second time just to the right side of his head. The third round was fired into the dirt between Jorge's spread knees.

Koral had shouted out involuntarily at the first report. The second and third came so quickly she could not respond. As the dust from the third shot gently sifted through the air back to the ground, and as Four rested the muzzle of the Kalashnikov against the hollow of Jorge's panting chest, Koral stumbled backward. She sat down with a muffled thump. She watched, eyes wide in shock, as Four leaned close to Jorge and began to speak, his voice amazingly calm.

"La dama es mi mujer. Si insultarla nuevo, te replantear, corte se abre y dejar que buitres que tiene." He straightened, only slightly, and continued. "Here's what you're going to do. You're going to tell Mr. Ham Deere to bring me a down payment in cash. Nothing bigger than hundreds and $100,000 will do. Meet me at 9 o'clock Monday night at the campfire site. He knows where it is. He comes alone. At that time we will negotiate when I get the rest of my half."

He stepped back, the muzzle of the AK47 still pointed at the trembling man. Four filled his lungs with air and spoke again.

"One more thing, Jorge. You tell Ham if there are any mines planted anywhere on my mountain come Monday, his share drops by half."

With a swiftness rivaling his attack on the drug mule, Four took apart the Kalashnikov, ripping off the magazine, ejecting the round in the chamber and removing the bolt. He threw each piece into the woods in a different direction. With the body of the rifle still tumbling through the underbrush, he grabbed Koral's hand and yanked her to her feet. Pulling her along, he headed swiftly back up the trail toward the creek.

After fifteen seconds—out of Jorge's hearing—he said, "Come on. We got to get out of here."

"Why?" She struggled to keep up with him. "That guy is afraid of you. Anyway, it'll take half an hour just to find and reassemble the piece."

"'Cause he ain't alone. No matter what he said. There will be lots of other grass patches just like that one, each with an armed guard. They all heard it when I fired those three rounds, and they are on their way now, sneaking through the brush. We need to be a mile down the creek when they get there."

Koral grew silent, focusing on the path before her. A feeling of nausea crept through her chest. Could it possibly be that she was now party to a large, hostile drug deal, the kind from which no one might simply walk away? She fought against an awful growing awareness that, in a single twenty-four hour period, she had found the love of her life and discovered him to be a ruthless, desperate criminal.

Chapter 6

She could not imagine a more placid, serene setting than the one she was experiencing: floating along the winding stream, just faster than the current, propelled by the sure, regular strokes of Four's paddle as it gently entered the clear water on alternating sides of the kayak. It was surreal. How could she be in such a pastoral, beautiful setting and feel such incredible, anxious dismay?

"You're trembling."

She did not turn toward him—this time because she didn't want him to see her face, to see how close she was to tears.

"Koral … I'm sorry I scared you so bad."

She dropped her head, her eyes closed. "I am scared, Four. What's going to happen to me?"

"To you? You aren't afraid of that guy, are you? Do you really think he's capable of hunting you up? …. Don't give him that much credit, Koral. He has no idea who you are or where you came from or what your relationship is to me."

She shook her head, tears coursing down her face. "I'm not talking about him. I'm talking about you."

"Me?" Genuine surprise was in his voice.

"I'm a party to a drug deal now. What are you going to do if you think I'm getting in the way of your transaction?"

Four was silent again for such a long period that she began to shiver. Koral could feel her heart pounding in her throat.

" … Koral, what you saw just now was the beginning of a sting."

She glanced over her shoulder. His eyes were on hers.

"A sting?"

"Do you remember Thursday in Trudy's diner? That man who came in and spoke to me and I got up and left?"

"Yes. Trudy said he was a state police officer."

"His name is Corbin Lester. He's the arresting officer who put my dad away."

"Yes, I know. Trudy told me."

"My dad had a partner, a guy named Ham Deere. Dad grew the grass and harvested it and turned it over to Deere's boys. Deere has always been an expert at keeping out of the legal crosshairs. The feds were after him when they ran afoul of Dad."

"What happened to your dad? He shot some people?"

He made a gruff sound, filled with exasperation. "The ATF tried to arrest Dad on weapons charges. The only thing was, they were listening to him with an unauthorized wiretap. After the shootout, when Dad and three feds ended up in adjoining hospital rooms down in Fayetteville, Corbin Lester came to see Dad.

"He laid out a plan where Dad got state time instead of federal. The feds, you know, have no parole. So instead of sixty years with no parole for the attempted murder of three federal agents, dad got twenty-one years for assault with a deadly weapon; that is, if he would plead guilty. With good behavior, he'll be out on parole in seven, about four more years. That lets the family keep their property. That also kept the feds from admitting they had illegal wiretaps."

Quietly he righted the kayak in the current and continued. "Apparently the state still wanted Deere, though. They've been watching him and the fellows who work for him. They somehow figured that marijuana was being grown on the mountain again, and they decided that I wasn't involved with it, so they decided I could help them catch Deere."

"Had they been following you?"

" ... I don't know how they knew I wasn't part of his operation. I'm paranoid enough that I can't imagine being followed without knowing it. Spend a little time in combat and you grow eyes in the back of your head." He shifted the paddle to the opposite side of the kayak to pull them back to the middle of the stream. "I'm thinking maybe they didn't know if I was involved and really they didn't care. I'm thinking Deere was the big fish they were after, and it didn't matter to them if I was involved, just so long as I was willing to drop a dime on him."

She waited for him to go on, trying to grasp how their encounter with the drug mule fit with what Four was being asked to do. "So what exactly do the police want from you?"

"Give them Ham Deere. That was why I set up the meeting for Monday night. When Deere meets me and hands over $100,000 in cash, that's like a de facto confession that the drugs are his."

"And you'll be wearing a microphone?"

"No. I don't want to risk that Deere would check me for it. As I understand it, the campfire meeting will be attended by camouflaged troopers."

"But what of Deere isn't alone?"

"I'd be surprised if he turned up alone. I just want him to think I think he'll be alone. And I'll have to rely on the police having superior numbers and proper positions."

She glanced over her shoulder. "Where is this campfire place?"

He grinned. "Why do you need to know that?"

Koral stared at the creek before them. "This just seems kind of dangerous to me …. So in return for helping them arrest Deere, they give you some kind of reward?"

"In return, they spring my daddy from the pen."

She gasped. "Really? They can do that?"

"Yep. That was the deal Corbin Lester came to offer me in the diner the other day. Said the governor would commute Dad's sentence to time served."

"And you said 'okay'?"

"I said I wanted it in writing. Lester said he couldn't do that. Said the governor's administration couldn't get actively involved in criminal stings. Said I'd have to take his word for it."

"So then you said 'okay'?"

"So then I said that wasn't good enough. Lester said he could get a recommendation for early release written by the sentencing judge addressed to the governor. He asked if that would be good enough. Then I said 'okay.' He's supposed to have it Monday morning, which is why I set the meet for Monday night."

She felt a growing awe, as well as real dread. "So all that happened just now … that was all by design to get a message to this guy Deere?"

"No. Not really. I thought I was going to have to go over to Hot Springs and hunt up one of his lackeys. Then, right there in the grass patch, the opportunity just presented itself. Jorge will have to tell Deere what I said, if for no other reason than that they can't ignore the way I walked right through their secure perimeter. In fact, I'm sure Deere already knows what happened."

"Well, not to spoil your plan or anything, but what if—instead of bringing you a sack of money on Monday—Deere sends some goons to look for you tonight?"

Four laughed. "Goons. I like that. Deere really can't do that. Mostly because he doesn't know who else knows what I know. Like I said to Jorge, as far as he is concerned, I have silent partners who will know exactly what to do if something happens to me."

She pursed her lips. "You must not be talking about me. I would have no idea what to do if something happened to you."

"Well ... I suppose you'd have to find somebody else to drive you down the mountain the next time your car dies."

She shook her head. "Not funny, Four Truett. This whole thing is so dangerous. My dad used to say, once shots are fired in a conflict, you've gone to the level where at least one side is going to lose."

"Yes, your dad is a smart man. I'm sorry I popped off those rounds like that. I just wanted Jorge and Deere to know that I was serious."

Koral cocked her head to one side. "Really?"

"Well, yeah. I was just trying to prove a point."

She looked back, her eyes fast on his. "And what was your point?"

" ... My point?"

"Yes, Four Truett. Exactly what were you trying to get across to poor Jorge?"

He shrugged. "Well, I just didn't want him to take me lightly."

Koral had grabbed hold of the formed edges of her bucket, so she could continue to face him. "Would this be a good time for me to tell you that I have a minor in Spanish? And that I lived in San Antonio for two years as a little girl, and my best friend, Gloria, spoke only Spanish in her home?"

" ... Yeah?"

"So I'm saying I know that not everything that transpired between you and Jorge was about selling marijuana."

He stared at her, wearing the expression of man wondering how much he should confess. " ... You know, with that rifle going off and all, I don't really remember what I said."

"Oh. Okay. As I recall, your friend looked at me and asked in Spanish, 'Who's the whore?' Then you knocked him on his ass, tore away his AK47, and fired three times in close proximity to his head and privates. And then you said to him, 'The lady is my woman. If you insult her again, I'll tie you down, cut you open, and leave you for the worms.'"

"Buzzards. I said 'buzzards.'"

"Ah. So you do remember."

"Some of it's coming back to me."

"Right. Well, I have a question about what you said to Mr. Jorge."

"Vazquez. *Senor* Jorge Vazquez."

"My question is: did you mean what you said about me, or was that part of your act to make him think you were crazy and pissed off?"

" … You kind of put me in a bind here, Koral. Either I have to say I was just sending up Jorge, or I have to say I'm in love with you."

"Yep. There's no flies on you, muscle boy." She sighed and turned back to the front of the boat. "It's a simple question. Did you mean what you said?"

She could hear the paddle dipping in the water, the rhythm smooth and placid.

"I'm not a guy who says things he doesn't mean, Koral. I didn't mean for you to hear it—not because I didn't mean it, just because … I don't know how to tell you how much you mean to me, how strong my feelings for you are."

She giggled.

"What?"

"You just did, Four Truett. You just told me exactly how you feel about me."

"It wasn't as bad as I expected."

"You mean at the security check?" Four said. "Yeah. Well, Dad's a trustee, plus they know me pretty well, although a couple of those guards at the admission gate looked like they wanted to give you a closer inspection."

Koral laughed. "Never in my life have I thought I was particularly attractive. Hearing you say things like that is totally new to me."

"You don't know your own strength, girly."

It was cool in the shade beneath the shelter in the picnic area. They sat side by side, waiting.

Koral recognized a growing anxiety within herself. Was it because she was within the confines of a prison? No. Was it a reluctance to meet Four's father because he was an inmate? No. She was nervous, she realized, because she didn't know if H. L. Truett III would approve of her.

"Your dad knows I was coming with you, right?"

"Well, kinda."

"Kinda. What do you mean, 'kinda'?"

"Well, he knows you exist."

" ... Knows I exist?"

He sighed and said slowly, "After I met up with the lawman on Thursday, I went home and called the prison. As a trustee, Dad has some phone privileges, so later he called me back. I told him I had something to talk to him about. His calls are all monitored, so I wasn't going to explain what I wanted to talk to him about today. And then, in the rest of our ten minutes, I kind of told him about you."

"What about me?"

"This must be your girl!" It was a man's voice, strong and surprising, similar to Four's, but older and a little gravelly.

Henry Truett sat down on the opposite side of the picnic table, staring at Koral, sizing her up, just as she was sizing him up. His hair had been dark brown in the past, though it had become salt-and-pepper gray. He was a handsome man, his face lined and pale. None of the Anglo prisoners she had seen that day had much of a tan. And he was smiling. From his expression he seemed to her to be a man who smiled a lot.

"Before I put my foot in my mouth," he said, "you are the one whose car broke down on the mountain, right?"

"Yes."

He seemed to be studying her face for something specific, looking from her hair to her chin and back. "She doesn't know, does she?"

"Know what?"

"Dad, this is Miss Koral Walker. Koral, this is Henry Louis Truett the Third."

"Hello, Koral." He extended his hand and shook hers as if greeting an equal. "You're every bit as lovely as my son said you were."

"Thank you." She felt herself blush. She looked down. "I'm sorry he didn't tell you I was coming today."

"I didn't know, Dad. She just showed up and insisted on coming along."

Her jaw dropped. "I did not!"

Henry laughed happily. "Four is just teasing. I'm glad for you to come along, Miss Walker. I think he's ashamed of most of his girlfriends."

"I am not. I just don't have any."

"Well, Koral is your girl, isn't she?"

Both of the men looked at her in silence. She stared back at them.

"I guess so. Yeah," she said.

"That's a relief." Four sighed. "I'd hate to bring somebody on a romantic outing like this, and she's not even willing to be my girlfriend."

They laughed together. A feeling of relief descended upon them. They had all, she realized, been anxious at the moment of meeting. The nervousness dissipated.

"What exactly did your son tell you about me, Mr. Truett?"

"Henry. Please do call me Henry. He called me a couple days ago and told me he was coming to see me. Then he told me about God answering his prayers."

"What?" Four's head tilted in surprise.

"Yep." Henry nodded. "Said a car broke down in front of him on Caddo Creek Road, and in it was the dream girl he'd been eyeballing since January. Said she was the most beautiful girl he'd ever seen."

" … Really, Henry? Are you making that part up?"

The older man studied her face silently, not so much trying to know what to say as trying to understand why she was asking. "Koral, when Four called me the other day and started talking about you, I knew from the sound of his voice that you were very pretty. And special … And a minute ago, when he was teasing about you showing up and tagging along? I haven't heard him do that in years. Not since before he went to Afghanistan."

She turned to Four. He was looking down at the picnic table. She could not read his expression.

"So what was it you wanted to talk to me about, son?"

"Getting you out of here. I was approached by a state lawman. They want me to help them with a sting. If I do—and if it works—they say they can translate that into early release. Real early."

95

Henry gazed at his son. "State lawman? Does this have something to do with Corbin Lester?"

Four nodded. "He's the one they sent to talk to me."

Slowly Henry Truett shook his head. "I had dealings with Corbin Lester. Now here I am behind the wall."

"The way I heard it, he kept you from getting federal time."

"I was stuck in a no-win situation, Four. You're not in any situation. I wouldn't trust the guy if I were you. Did you get the deal in writing?"

"No. They say if they put it in writing, they don't know who all might see it. The documents are supposed to come from the governor, though, as soon as the deal goes down."

"And what is the deal? What are they asking you to do?"

This time it was Four shaking his head. "I don't know who's listening, Dad."

" … It just don't feel righteous to me, Four."

"You haven't asked me what's in it for you."

"I'm more interested in what you're getting yourself into."

"A full pardon. Recommended by the Board of Corrections and signed by the governor. You could walk out of here a free man within the month. You don't think that sounds righteous?"

"It sounds too good to be true." Henry nodded toward Koral. "Look at all what you got going for you, son. You're going to graduate soon. You got the best-looking girl in two states."

Again she felt herself blush.

"And all those orchards you been planting. They'll be bearing big time. The mountain is going to be a garden."

"This deal will secure the whole mountain for us forever, Dad."

Henry's brow furled. His eyes shone with recognition. "So that's it. The whole mountain, you say?" His voice dropped to the point it was scarcely audible. "My old partner is back growing on Truett Mountain, isn't he?"

"I never said that. But if he was, wouldn't you want him to finally carry his share of the burden? He was always the big game they were going after."

"His time is coming. I won't be in here forever. But when I hear Ham is involved in this, it just sounds that much more dangerous."

Four shrugged. "If he don't have an RPG, I'll be just fine."

Henry laughed. "That's my boy all right." He glanced at Koral.

"So, Miss Walker, Four came to ask my permission to work a sting to get me out of here. Well, getting out of here is something that's going to happen for me eventually anyway. I'm going to say this to him in front of you in case he gets forgetful. Then you can remind him."

He drew a breath and faced Four. "Son, under no circumstances are you to enter into an arrangement with Corbin Lester on my behalf. Under no circumstance are you to try to get Ham Deere in a sting. He's the most dangerous man I know. When you walk out through that trap gate—before you get to your Camaro—you call Lester and tell him you changed your mind."

Four leaned back. "Okay, Dad. If you feel that way about it."

"I do. And that's the end of it." He stood abruptly. "Miss Walker—Koral, it's very nice to meet you. You come back and visit me anytime." He tilted his head toward Four. "Bring him if you want to."

With that, hands in his pockets, he turned and walked away.

After he disappeared through the trap gate into the corrections building, she looked at Four. "Just like that the deal is off?"

"Oh hell no. I'm the guy who drives Hummers into firefights against orders, remember." He stood. "Anybody else here you want to see?"

"Uh, no."

"Well, let's get going."

He held out his hand and she grasped it. It occurred to her, as they walked through the gate, the admissions building, and across the parking lot, that she had not held hands with a boy since she was in high school.

Buckling in and listening to the familiar, satisfying rumble of the Camaro's engine, her mind flitted from one awareness to another. What did it mean that Four was going ahead with the sting to trap Ham Deere? What made Henry Truett afraid for his son, so afraid he would refuse a chance to get out of prison four years before his first chance at parole? Besides keeping silent, what could she do to help Four, or was she foolish and immature to even think of helping him? … And what did Henry mean when he said, 'She doesn't know, does she'?"

"What did your dad mean?"

"What?"

"Your dad said, 'She doesn't know, does she?' What was he talking about, Four?"

He gazed down the road, his jaw set. "Well, Miss Walker, it's time for you to meet my aunt."

Chapter 7

Aunt Eleanor's house was in a part of Fayetteville that Koral had never seen. The homes were brick and frame, two-story, and well-shaded with mature oaks, elms and maples. The roads were curved and hilly and the area exuded an air of understated wealth.

"Are you sure your aunt is going to be okay with us just showing up like this?" she asked.

"What time is it? Four-thirty? She's going to think we're manna from heaven."

"Why is that?"

"'Cause she can cook for us."

Four pulled into the driveway of a smaller, well-kept home. A white-railed porch ran the length of the front, and azaleas, just ready to bloom, adorned the yard in front of the porch. The wood siding—at least what could be seen of it beneath the overhang of the roof—was a pleasant yellow.

"Come on, Miss Walker. Time for you to meet the high-class member of our family."

Koral was conscious of him placing her in front as they walked up the sidewalk and wooden steps. He had her stand immediately before the door, himself a half-step behind her as he rang the bell. Her anxiety rose suddenly, sharply, but only for an instant. That was all it took for the front door to swing open.

Before her stood a lovely, auburn-haired woman in her late fifties or early sixties, wearing an old-fashioned A-line dress. She radiated graciousness and welcome before she spoke a word. And an instant after she opened the door, her expression was transformed with delight.

"Aunt Eleanor, this is Koral Walker."

"Come in this house this instant." Eleanor reached out and pulled Koral to her, first in a tight embrace and then locking their arms as they walked through her entry together. "You must be the beauty who has been seen in the company of Four Truett around these parts the last few days. I'm his Aunt Eleanor, Koral. I'm so glad to meet you."

"I'm glad to meet you."

"And has he told you about the great family resemblance you bear?"

She looked over her shoulder at Four, trailing them through the house. "No ma'am. That must be what Henry was referring to."

"Oh. You met my baby brother." This time it was Eleanor looking back at Four. "Seems as if my nephew is introducing you to his whole family. This must be serious."

Something in her chest fluttered. She wanted to say it couldn't be serious yet, that they scarcely knew one another. Yet in truth it was serious. In the last few hours she had become involved in complex ways—with drug lords and police stings—beyond anything she had ever experienced. Then there came to her the flash of a memory of the two of them tangled naked in his bed, desperate to satisfy their shared craving. Yes, it was serious.

Eleanor stopped in the sunny dining room, standing before a wall that apparently served as a family portrait gallery. Immediately before Koral, just at eye level, was an old black-and-white photograph. She leaned forward in amazement at what appeared to be an image of herself. The woman in the photo seemed a few years older than Koral and perhaps more petite. She wore a dress suited to the early 20th century and had long hair pinned close to her head. Her features, from the round, inquisitive eyes to the short, pert nose and oval face, was virtually Koral Walker. She felt her hand rise slowly to the glass, then draw back.

"It's my grandmother, my namesake. Eleanor."

"We look so much alike."

"Exactly alike to my eye. Eleanor was her given name, but she went by Lacey. Lacey Warren."

"Is she—"

"She died long before I was born. She is sort of a mystery person. She married Grandpa Andy when she was twenty-six or so, but it's like she just suddenly appeared out of nowhere on his mountain."

"His mountain? Caddo Creek?"

"No, they lived in North Carolina, up in the Blue Ridge Mountains near a little town called Boone."

Koral nodded. "I know about Boone. Appalachian State University is there."

"Yes. Lacey and Andy had one child, my mother Elizabeth. And Lacey died of cancer when Mom was in her late teens." She looked at her nephew. "I hope you two came hungry."

He nodded. "We did, ma'am."

Eleanor put her hands on his shoulders, physically moving him backward in the direction of the front door. "Well, then, here's what you need to do, son. Go down to the grocery store. Not the one at the bottom of the hill. I mean the one over by—"

"Townsend's Market?"

"Yes. You're a smart boy. Because?"

"Because they have Pillsbury flour?"

"Self-rising. Might as well get me two sacks. You don't need any money, do you?"

"Uh, no ma'am."

"Good. Get going before we starve."

Studying the other photos on the dining room wall, Koral tried—unsuccessfully—to suppress a smile. She heard the front door open and close, then felt Eleanor standing beside her again.

"He seems to do just what you tell him."

"He'd better. That's how he was raised. And he'd better hop to and show that same respect to you."

"Actually he is very polite and respectful."

"Good." Eleanor tapped the glass on the portrait of her grandmother. "She was a prostitute."

Koral turned to the older woman. "Excuse me?"

"Yep. She was working in a cathouse all right. That bit of information has been passed down from one woman to another. Supposedly none of the men in the family know it."

"Really? She was a …"

"That's what my momma told me. And Lacey told her. Grandpa Andy was a World War I veteran. His first wife, Lib, died in childbirth. Sometime after that, he stopped off at a place in the North Carolina piedmont for a meal, as the story goes, not realizing it was a whorehouse. As I heard it, Lacey was drunk and passed out, and he kidnapped her."

"Kidnapped her?"

"Um hmm. Threw her over his shoulder and just carried her out.

The fellow who ran the place tried to stop him, and Grandpa whipped out a big pistol and backed him off. Then he drove her right up his mountain and sobered her up. After that, she fell in love with him."

"That's—that's amazing."

"I think it's romantic as hell," Eleanor said, her hands on her hips. "Makes me wet just thinking about it. Want to help me fix supper?"

"Uh. Yes. Of course."

Eleanor took her by the arm and guided her through the doorway into the spacious, bright kitchen. Koral knew immediately she was in over her head.

"Eleanor, I have to confess I'm not much of a cook."

"Nobody is born knowing how to cook, sweetie," the older woman replied, not hesitating as she opened cabinets and cupboards, pulling out pans, spices and utensils. "You keep coming over here and I'll teach you everything you need to know. The surest way to get a Truett man to do what you want is to feed him a good meal."

Koral smiled. "That's just what Trudy said."

"Marvin's wife?" She handed a small pot to Koral. "Fill that a third of the way with water, will you? Isn't Trudy a treasure? Best thing that ever happened to my moron nephew."

She laughed. "Your family is so much fun."

"We're just folks. Now set it on to boil. Turn the burner up about three-quarters."

"Can I ask you a question?"

"Sure, sweetie. Anything you want."

"Well, how come you're trusting me with all this personal information, like family secrets? And you're telling me to come over and learn to cook. You just met me. Why are you sharing all this with me?"

Eleanor stopped and faced her. "Koral, the moment I opened the door, I saw you were the living embodiment of my grandma I never met."

"Yeah but looks can be—"

"That's not why I love you," she said, shaking her head. "You see, I was watching Four's face when he called your name. I've seen that look before, but not on that young man. I knew right then you were the one."

"But … he and I just met. Really."

"Maybe so." She smiled coyly. "But I bet you know each other very well."

The sudden movement beside Koral woke her. In that instant she realized again how much her life had changed. Richard had never spent the entire night in her room, nor she in his. But she had slept the previous night through in Four's bed and tonight he was in hers. And this was the second night in her entire life she had slept in the nude.

They had fallen asleep after making love and left a light burning somewhere in her apartment. In the dimness she could see his form stretched beside her. He jerked again. Some utterance she did not understand came from his lips. He jumped, turning onto his back, his body taut. She realized he was having a night terror. And she did not know what to do. Still she did respond, from somewhere deep within her, an intuitive place beyond her conscious self.

Koral rolled onto her side facing Four and, without putting her arms around him, pressed gently against him along the full length of his body. In that instant, there seemed a momentary relaxation of his frame, a pause in his inner panic. She brushed his cheek with the back of her hand and whispered his name. He stopped the jerking motions, as if waiting for something, some further orders or some new clarity.

"Four," she said again. "It's Koral. You're all right. You're in bed with me in my apartment. You're all right, my love." Kissing his cheek, she rubbed against his side, pressing her breast against his shoulder, opening her legs so her pubis was against his thigh.

He seemed to sigh. She couldn't tell if he had slipped back into sleep or was waking. The outline of his face turned from her. Then his shoulders began to quiver slightly. He was weeping. Koral put her hand against his face again.

He swallowed. "Did I hurt you?"

"No. Of course not." Her voice was strange to her. It had a soft, assuring tone she did not know she possessed.

Four's shoulders began to shake. He sobbed for a full minute. Koral said nothing, simply placing her face against his arm.

At length he drew a long, quivering breath. "I'm so sorry …. This is why, you see? This is why I can't be with you. I'm broken,

Koral. I'm just a derelict." He wiped his eyes with the back of a hand. "Don't you see?"

"No," she replied in the calm, healing voice she had newly acquired. "Explain it to me, Four."

He sighed deeply. "I can't stop them, no matter how hard I try. Seems like every time I have a really good day, one of these awful dreams just slaps the hell out of me. It's like, 'Don't enjoy your life. You don't deserve it and you know it'."

"Um hmm," she comforted. "Don't you think the good that happens when you're awake is just as important as the bad dreams that come when you're asleep?"

He thought about her words. At length he propped himself up on his elbows, staring into the darkness at the foot of the bed.

"They're just so real."

She nodded. "I could tell."

" ... Did I scare you?"

"I was only scared that I couldn't help you."

Four took another deep breath. "You did help." He smiled. "Nobody ever woke me up from one of those before. I like the way you did it."

She propped her head on her wrist. "I just used what I had available at the time."

Four studied her face. Because the dull light source was at his back, he could see her better than she could see him.

"What about the next one I have? What am I supposed to do when we aren't sleeping naked in the same bed?"

"Well ... maybe that's just a real good reason for you not to lose interest in me."

"Lose interest in you? Just what about you do you think I'll lose interest in first? Will it be your genius little brain with your unlimited knowledge of things like horticulture, small arms, and classic movies? Or maybe I'll get bored by your incredibly loveable personality and wit and ability to interact easily with all the strange people—like my family—you meet. And what was it my dad said? Oh yeah, you're the prettiest girl in two states. Maybe I'll get tired of the way you look."

"What about the way I make love?" Koral interjected. "Don't you think I'm kind of amateurish?"

She could tell he was staring at her, was able to see her face better than she could see his. She could not, however, make out his expression. And for an instant she wondered if she had asked the wrong question, if his silence was the answer.

Then he reached for her. He pulled her all the way on top of him and kissed her. Laying his head back on the pillow, he lifted her shoulders gently and moved her upward so that, as he lowered her, his mouth covered a breast. Instantly Koral felt herself relax and grow aroused.

"Not everything in the night is a terror, Four." Her voice was soft. It had the slightest note of pleading, yearning in it.

He sucked her breast deeply into his mouth, rolling his rough tongue over and around the nipple. The sensation caused her to arch her back and close her eyes. She felt him sigh.

"Your tits are like ice cream cones." He cupped his hands gently around them. "Succulent. Sweet ... And they don't melt."

"What flavor?"

"Oh. They start as creamy vanilla. Then, as we make love and sweat all over each other, they become Butter Brickle."

She felt his member thicken and begin to straighten along the inside of her thigh. Without conscious intention, her legs widened and she slid down his body. He moved his hands from her breasts to her buttocks, pressing her against him, his erect penis teasingly lying partly within the wet lips of her vagina. In the dim light she recognized he was smiling.

"It feels so good." His voice was quiet. "You're right. Everything in the night isn't a terror."

Koral pulled her knees forward until she was sitting on the upper part of his thighs. Then, reaching down, she lifted his stiffened penis and ran the glans upward against the layered flesh beneath her clitoris. She forced the two against each other, rubbing them together, then holding them apart. Warm effluence flowed over her fingers ... hers or his, she wondered—before realizing how wet each was.

She slid the cock into her passage slowly, bowing her back to put extra pressure on him. From Four's reaction, she could tell the arousing effect it had. With an agonizing slowness, she raised and lowered herself on the engorged shaft again and again. Motionless beneath her, he moaned.

Her voice was triumphant, dominant even in its husky quietness.

"You are under my control. You belong to me, love slave."

" ... What are going to do with me?"

"What am I going to do with you?" Koral tightened her inner walls on him. Her voice became a fierce whisper. "I'm going to squeeze every drop of cum out of you and make you beg for mercy."

His eyes closed, Four put his hands on her hips and began to arch upward in a rhythm matching her downward stroke. "Let me help you with that."

Gradually the pulse of their moving together, his penis disappearing fully within her, quickened. Koral closed her eyes and raised her chin, tilting her head back as far as it would go, increasing the fiction on her clitoris. She could feel the orgasm approach—tantalizing, beckoning—until the sweet moment it became inevitable. Intentionally she slowed the dipping of her body onto Four to prolong the orgasm. She gazed down at his face, thirsty to make him climax in the same instant.

She reached forward and pinched both his nipples and pressed hard on his penis with her inner lips at the very instant he began his urgent upward pounding into her. His fingers tightened on her and his thrusts seemed desperate. He gave a little cry. Koral was so intent in watching him come that she was surprised by the swiftness and intensity of her own orgasm—the electric spasm through her passage and up her back. And for an instant she ceased all movement. She sat astride him—the only sound their ragged breathing, the only sensation the throbbing of his disengorged, expended member still within her.

Koral fell forward onto his chest, her arms across the pillows, her cheek against his hot cheek. As her body relaxed, she felt the slow flood of all they had produced together pouring forth onto Four, his genitals awash in their warm cream.

She breathed deeply. "What good is it to squeeze all the cum out of you if I'm just going to drip it all back onto you?"

"Well." His breath was halting, exerted. "You'll just have to keep practicing and try to do better .... No more of this making me pop helplessly with all this amateurish hot sex and those irresistible simultaneous orgasms. You have to ... do a lot of research and figure out what you're supposed to be doing .... But, seriously, if this gets any more arousing, I'm a dead man."

She lay silently, feeling his breathing and the pounding of his heart against her breasts. A lovely tranquility descended upon her and then a childlike capriciousness.

"If you found me drunk and helpless, would you kidnap me and take me up on your mountain and sober me up and make me fall in love with you?"

He chuckled. "Oh. You mean the way Grandpa Andy did with Grandma Lacey?"

She raised her head and looked at him. "You know about that?"

"About Lacey being a whore and Andy sobering her up and marrying her? Everybody in the family knows that."

"Eleanor said only the women know."

"Um hmm. Sounds to me like only the men can keep a secret."

"Hmm." She put her head back on his chest. "I think I should tell your Aunt Eleanor. She's such a delightful person."

"She is topflight in every way. She's the best person, the toughest person, and a real survivor. How'd you like her hair?"

"Her hair? It was okay, I guess. I didn't really notice. Why?"

"'Cause it's a wig. That was her natural hair color all right, but she just finished two months of chemo. Stage three breast cancer." He shook his head. "But you would never know, would you?"

"She invited me to come over. She said she would teach me how to cook for you … so you really will be my helpless love slave."

Even in the dim light, she could make out his broad smile. "It's a little too late for that, Auntie."

She scooted down and put her hands together on his chest and rested her chin on them. Four in turn put his hands behind his head his elbows extended across their pillows.

"You know, this is only Sunday," she said. "We have seven days of spring break in front of us. We haven't talked about it all. Do you have plans? Things you need to do? …. I don't mean to presume. I was thinking maybe I could come up on the mountain and stay with you. If that's okay."

Once again she could not gauge from his silence or his expression in the darkness how he was responding to her question. A minute passed before he spoke.

"There is nothing in the world I would like more than to spend the week on the mountain with you, Miss Walker. Only, let me get past tomorrow night. Then we'll make plans for the week."

Images of Four ripping the AK-47 away from Jorge Vasquez

flashed through Koral's mind. Suddenly she was very frightened at the prospect, the unpredictable danger of the drug sting in which he was to participate.

"You know, your dad doesn't want you to do that, Four. He doesn't trust that state policeman."

He nodded slowly. "I don't trust Corbin Lester either. But he has what I need to get my dad out of prison. And it sounds like the police need me more than I need them."

She considered her words carefully. "You need back-up. Somebody who can shoot."

"Ha, girl! If you think I'm letting you anywhere near the mountain tomorrow night, you're fucking crazy."

"So where is this meeting taking place?"

He shook his head. "You have no need of knowing, Miss Walker."

" … I'm scared, Four."

He drew a breath. "Let me tell you exactly what's going to happen. Tomorrow morning I'm taking you up to Caddo Creek to fetch your car. You're going to drive back down here and have a nice relaxing evening. Then Tuesday afternoon or thereabouts, I'll call you. We'll plan out the rest of the week." He paused, waiting for her to comment. "So let's talk about something pleasant. Like the way you feel—naked, wet and beautiful—lying on top of me."

Chapter 8

By the time Koral pulled her Celica to a stop before her apartment, she had decided precisely what she intended to do.

Long after Four drifted off to serene sleep, she had been awake, brooding. The drug sting, as she recalled from what she had heard as they paddled down Caddo Creek Saturday morning, depended on a lot of trust—and it depended on everything coming off just as planned with perfect timing. Four had to count on Corbin Lester being present and hidden when Ham Deere, the drug lord, implicated himself. He had to count on Deere's willingness to deal Four in as a partner. She thought about the anti-personnel mines planted on the mountain, about the AK-47 Vasquez had been carrying. It was difficult for her to believe Deere would simply give in and share his ruthlessly guarded profits over nothing more compelling than a threat from Four Truett.

Even beyond her doubts about the logistics of the sting, she was nagged by a feeling of dread she could not shake. Surely Four had the same wariness. It was his desire to free his father—coupled with his abundant recklessness, his quick willingness to risk his own wellbeing for the wellbeing of those he valued—that drove him into taking this great chance. She was not willing to let him take such a great risk … at least not alone.

Neither of them had spoken much in the morning. She had fixed oatmeal and instant orange juice for their late breakfast, trying to joke about her inadequacy in the kitchen. Four had tried unsuccessfully as well to present a light-hearted front. There was a distance to his silence she had not experienced.

Almost nothing was said during the hour-long drive up the mountain. Koral stared out the open passenger window of the Camaro, her lungs filled with pure, sweet air, the throb of the engine becoming almost a meditative chant.

When they stopped on his driveway next to her little Toyota, she got out immediately, walked to her car and opened the driver's door.

"So you're going to call me tomorrow? First thing?"

He had nodded. "Soon as I wake up. I'll tell you how everything went."

Koral slid into the front seat. "Well, good luck."

"You're not sore, are you—" He took a step toward her. "—about not coming along tonight?"

She shook her head. "Not if you're going to tell me what happens. And please be very careful."

Four had said something else, but she had stopped listening. She backed around and drove off his property and down to Fayetteville.

After she entered her apartment, she locked her front door and closed the bedroom door behind her as well. Dropping onto her knees beside the bed, she felt along the underside of the metal frame until she found the rectangular outline. The latches popped open in her fingers and she gingerly lowered the black steel box to the floor. Snug inside was the walnut case.

Koral fitted the tiny brass key into the lock and opened it and raised the cover. The aromas of felt, furniture polish and lubricating oil rose to her nostrils. It took only a few seconds for her to assemble the antique Browning .22 Challenger. She gripped it and maneuvered it in her hands, reacquainting herself with the heft and the smoothness of it. Along the bottom of the long barrel she attached the laser site and turned it on. At the slight movement of her hand, a crisp red dot ran along the wall and ceiling of her bedroom. She turned off the laser.

Sitting with her back against her bed, she took both clips and began to load them with rim fire long rifle rounds. It brought back to her memory the evening her father had given her the prized pistol in celebration of her certification as a handgun expert.

"Now, Koral—" He had spoken deliberately as he demonstrated how to disassemble and clean the weapon, and as she sat watching, rapt. "—rumor has it this is the most accurate automatic sidearm ever mass-produced. I will tell you, however, no piece is accurate if the shooter isn't."

What would it do to her accuracy, she wondered, if this night for the first time she were to shoot at a human being? What if the life of this man she loved were in the balance? What if someone were shooting at her?

Koral made no noise as she climbed the steps of the deck behind the house and peered through Trudy's kitchen window. The faint, fading daylight made it easy to see Trudy standing within at the sink and Marvin sitting at the table, stretched backward in his chair, talking to her. The soft tapping on the back door clearly surprised them. They looked first at the door, then at each other, then back to the door.

Marvin stood and gingerly opened it. The sight of Koral standing on the deck, dressed completely in black, seemed to baffle him. As he stood staring at her in silence, Trudy joined him.

"Are the girls in bed?" Koral asked.

Trudy nodded. "Yes."

"Good. I need you to drive me somewhere, Marvin."

"Did your car break down again?" he asked.

"No. I need you to drive me somewhere secret and drop me off."

He turned instantly. "Let me get my keys."

Trudy remained, staring at her, bewildered. She put her hands on her hips. "This is about Four Truett, I expect."

"Yes."

"Well, Koral, honey, I can tell you anything you want to know about him. You don't have to go sneaking around. He don't have no other—"

"No, Trudy. This isn't a checking-up-on-him thing. This is a keeping-him-from-getting-shot thing."

"Oh ... Well, what do you need us to do?"

Marvin came back into the kitchen, keys in hand.

"Just this," Koral said quietly.

She turned and walked down the steps. The wood sagged at the weight of Marvin behind her. They walked around the house to the driveway, where Koral's car was parked behind his shop truck.

"Follow me to Four's."

She slid into her car, watching from the corner of her eye to make sure Marvin did as she told him. They pulled down the drive onto the mountain road.

Koral glanced at the face of her watch. It was 8:15. The sky was almost completely dark.

Marvin was still close behind her as she veered onto the long drive to Four's house. She pulled across the Caddo Creek bridge and up to the house. Matilda, lying on the front steps, recognized both vehicles—and the two drivers who emerged from them—and offered nothing more than casual observation.

"Four ain't here."

"I didn't expect him to be," she replied. "I want to leave my car here and for you to take me to him."

Marvin's face for the first time showed resistance. "I don't have no idea where he is, Miss Walker. What's this all about?"

She had walked around to the passenger's door and pulled out a black duffel bag through the window.

"Let's just suppose that tonight at nine o'clock Four was going to meet a drug boss somewhere on the mountain. Where would that be?"

"The fire pit at the higher crossroads," he said quietly. "Is he in trouble?"

"He doesn't think so." She opened the passenger door of the truck and pulled herself into the cab. "Christ, Marvin, is this supposed to be a rolling toolbox or a junk metal bin? Anyway, Four's dad said he didn't trust the cops involved."

Marvin climbed back into the truck, his expression dark. "Must have something to do with Corbin Lester."

"Yes. And Henry's old partner."

"Hamilton Deere." He rested his great palms on the steering wheel. "That makes me nervous, too." He glanced at her. "What are you intending to do?"

"I just want to watch Four's back. He thinks he's got it under control. I just want to be there to make sure. If the sting works like it's supposed to, he won't even know I'm there. How close can you get me to that crossroads without us being seen or heard?"

Marvin deliberated. "Half a mile. Maybe less than that. I can take you up through the west pasture. From there I can tell you how to get to the crossroads easy." He started the engine. "Don't you think I should go get my new rifle and come along with you?"

She shook her head. "Really, I'm sort of trained for this. And, nothing personal, but you're kind of a big target."

They continued up the drive, circling above the house and up the mountain. In a moment she saw the outline of the greenhouse in the peach orchard where she and Four first made love. A stab of fear threatened to close her throat.

Koral responded by opening her bag and taking out the black

holster. As she had been drilled to do, she checked the Velcro pouches for the equipment she needed and strapped on the holster. She lifted the target pistol free and slid a loaded clip into the handle. Then she produced night-vision goggles, pulled them into place, and lifted the lenses from in front of her eyes.

Marvin shook his head at the display of hardware and her ease with it. "You're a commando."

"No, cousin. I always wear underwear. Tonight it just happens to be black."

When he did not laugh or reply, she glanced at him and smiled. "I'm sorry," she said. "'Going commando' is slang for not wearing underwear."

"Oh." He chuckled. "You miss out on a lot when you don't go to college, I guess. So what do you want me to do after I drop you off?"

Koral stared down at the camouflage putty in her hand.

"Just go home," she said. "Nobody knows you heard anything about this. You and Trudy and the girls are safe that way, just in case the drug guy goes over the top. That's why I parked my car at Four's house instead of yours. You and Trudy just need to lay low."

Marvin pulled off the gravel road and headed across rutted pasture land. He shook his head.

"No, Miss Walker. I reckon this is a family thing now. My cousin wouldn't just leave me up here on the mountain and pretend he didn't know I needed help." Marvin gripped the wheel. "And you doing this for Four ... this pretty much makes you family."

They bumped across the fields in silence. She didn't know what else she could say. The strength of Marvin's declaration overwhelmed her. She did feel that she belonged to the Truetts. And they belonged to her.

He turned along fence rows and up unseen paths. Soon he slowed and began to use his parking lights. Three deer bounded away from them at the last moment as they drove carefully across a field that inclined before them. Marvin pulled close to the tree line at the far end of the meadow and shut off the engine. Koral silently covered the rest of her exposed flesh with camo and pulled on dull black leather gloves. When she was finished, she sat, looking down, her hand on the door handle.

"I really love your family, Marvin. I love all the Truetts. You've been good to me."

"Oh you haven't seen nothing yet. You act like you aren't going to get the full treatment."

She glanced up at him.

"I'll be right here, waiting for you. As long as it takes. Just walk straight ahead. There's a series of ridges and swales nobody can drive across. Then about 500 yards in, it smooths out and you come to an intersection of three little roads. There's a level circle where they meet. But half the circle is ringed heavy with trees."

"That's perfect. Thanks."

Koral shouldered the heavy door, opening it as quietly as she could. She leaned against it to close it. Then she lowered the goggles. The meadow around her and the woods before shimmered in green light as she maneuvered through them.

She was surprised by the realization that she was still able to recognize the various species of shrubs, trees, vines and undergrowth she was walking through. Equally surprising were the night birds and insects dipping and bursting through the dark air, though the only sound came from the grasses and weeds brushing her pant legs.

Just as Marvin had described, the terrain was folded into a series of steep, narrow washes. Cattle paths marked the easiest passages through them. Soon she heard her soft exerted breathing. There were four, then five swales to traverse. As she climbed to the top of the fifth, she became aware of a clearing before her to her right. She stopped instantly and held her breath.

Forty yards away were the crossroads, the intersection of three rutted paths. And where they met, a light-colored circle devoid of vegetation. Parked long ways at the circle, leaning against the grill of his Camaro was the unmistakable form of Four Truett. He stood with his back to her, wearing a flannel shirt—open, untucked. Koral had never seen him wear his shirt outside his pants, not even a T-shirt. Then, as she watched, she saw him slide his right hand along the inside of his shirt in the back and rest it there for a moment, gripping something and then letting go.

"Ah, so you are packing a piece, muscle boy," she whispered. "But I have to get closer."

She surveyed the area carefully. Four was watching one road, obviously expecting Deere's car to come from that path. The tree line and woods Marvin described began fifty yards to her left, and there Koral saw the outline of a second car.

It was a big Ford, a Crown Vic. That was the car Corbin Lester had been driving Thursday when he came into the diner to speak to Four. While she could easily make out the car, its position behind the trees and a few feet lower than the meeting circle made it invisible to anyone at the crossroads. She—and perhaps Four—had expected more than one police car. Perhaps tonight they would only listen and not try to arrest the drug lord.

"Well, so far so good," she whispered. "Maybe this will happen like it's supposed to."

She lowered herself into the wash and checked her watch: 8:50. Then she began the slow work of moving along the natural terrace toward the sheltering trees. A rabbit heard her when she was five feet from it. It stood up on its hind legs facing her, its ears erect. She realized then that she was virtually invisible. It turned and loped away silently as she moved toward it.

The terraced walls gradually descended. Koral slowly crouched and then went to her hands and knees. The Crown Vic was clear in her vision, twenty feet away. From this point, though, she had no view of the circle. She moved through the undergrowth incrementally—one elbow, then the opposite knee. And then she found herself staring between two maple saplings, the crossroads plainly in sight, Four's rear bumper only fifteen feet away. She could see him, at the opposite end of the car, from the waist up.

Then came the rumbling sound of another vehicle. Its lights shone in the treetops, blindingly brilliant. She flipped up the goggles. The SUV emerged from the path Four had been watching. It stopped with a jerk at the edge of the circle, the headlights remaining on for illumination even as the engine was turned off. She saw Four raise a hand briefly to shield his eyes. What sort of vehicle was it? Squinting, she made out the name "Range Rover."

For half a minute, nothing happened. She slipped the Challenger from her holster. Silently she reached a gloved hand inside her collar and pulled out the black mp3 player strung around her neck. She pressed a button. The momentary red dot indicated it was on and recording.

The driver's door opened and a man stepped out. He came around in the full illumination of the headlights, his hands free and his gait completely casual.

It was the first time Koral had seen this man, Hamilton Deere, whom so many had discussed. He was slender and not overly tall, wearing casual office clothes. She was surprised at how handsome he was and how disarmingly unconcerned he seemed.

"Hello, Four."

"Ham. You by yourself?"

"Sure. Just like you said …. Well, you asked for this meeting. Something you want to talk about?"

"You being here—does that mean you accept my offer?"

"What offer would that be?"

Four sighed, his jaw tight. "Do you really want to dick with me? 'Cause if you do, tomorrow morning I'm taking my brush hog to the fallow pasture on top of the mountain and cut down everything growing there. And as I do, I'll use the sprayer and 'Round Up' the whole field. And if I find anybody up there who doesn't belong, I'll kill 'em…. So, if you don't know what I'm talking about, our meeting is over and you can shag your ass off my mountain."

Twice before, Koral had heard the tone in Four's voice, once when warning the deputy and once when confronting the drug mule. There was no denying the underlying menace, certainty and seriousness in it. She had to remind herself this was part of the sting, that he was only saying this to prompt the drug lord to admit the acres of marijuana were his. Still, his words were true. He really did want to plow under the plants and drive away the intruders.

Deere's face remained completely emotionless, so much so that Koral wondered if he had not heard or understood what had been said to him. Then he broke into a smile—childlike and bright. And in that instant she realized the depth of his ruthless evil. She recognized his every action and motive was to further his own ends and protect himself, and that he could not be trusted in any way.

"Four," he said, shaking his head, "you're so like your dad. I love your dad. I would have helped him too—anyway I could, if I could have done it without giving anybody the idea he was my partner. So I'm glad to cut you in. And maybe I can help him by helping you."

Four laughed. "Cut me in? What bullshit. Fifty-fifty. An even split. And don't ever call me your 'partner'. Bad things happen to your partners."

As Deere paused, considering his response, Koral idly wondered how Four would know if he were getting half the money for the sale of the marijuana.

"That's kind of like blackmail, isn't it, Four? Fifty percent just for not ruining my operation? You didn't plant it. You didn't cultivate it. You aren't going to harvest, transport or distribute it. You're asking for an awful big cut of the action just to keep your mouth shut."

Was that an admission, Koral wondered. Was Corbin Lester listening and had he heard enough to file charges against Deere?

"This isn't a negotiation. Take half or get nothing. And after this crop, cultivate your shit somewhere else."

He was smiling again. "Four, you have the best land for this mountain-grown crop in the whole Southwest. This could be a long-term, longtime benefit for both of us. Ha. I don't know about that fifty percent, though."

"That's fine, Ham. Then we're through here." He stepped toward the door of the Camaro.

"Hold on. Hold on." For the first time there was a hint of urgency in Deere's voice. "Here's what I can do …. I'll give you a quarter million up front. Cash money. Then I can give you more a week after I move it, up to a third."

Four stared at him. "Thirty-five percent. All cash. No bills larger than hundreds."

"Deal." Deere smiled broadly. "And after this crop, we can talk about a fall planting. We should shake on it." He extended his hand, smiling.

"I'm good." Four raised his palm as if holding Deere at bay.

A car engine started. It was the Crown Vic. Both men in the clearing jumped, turning toward the noise. Koral could see the outline of the car to her left as it pulled forward, climbing the little berm up to the edge of the tree line. The headlights cut on, shining down on Four and Ham Deere.

Koral focused on Deere, lifting the Browning pistol, waiting to see if he would produce a weapon. Instead he shielded his eyes. He seemed to remain calm, unperturbed. Even confronted with the possibility of arrest, he betrayed no concern.

The light inside the Crown Vic came on as the driver's door popped open. Corbin Lester stepped out, leaving the door open, and walked around the front of the car down to the crossroads.

"What have we got here?" His voice was loud, triumphant. "Looks like a couple drug dealers partnering up. I guess I got here just in time, didn't I?"

Deere stared at him wordlessly.

"Did you get it?" Four asked. "Were you taping it?"

"I didn't tape anything, Truett. Didn't need to. I was just waiting for Ham to hold out his hand. Meant the deal was done."

Four's head snapped toward the officer. "You were waiting for him to give you a signal?"

Koral felt her grip tighten on the pistol.

"Relax," Lester said. "Let's jawbone." When Four said nothing, he continued. "I like the chemistry of our little group here, don't you?"

"Our little group?"

"C'mon, Four," Deere said. "Do you really think I'm dumb enough to fall for a sting? If you tried to do something like that to me, I'd kill you."

He looked from one man to the other. "So what is going on here? The joke's on me?"

"No," Deere said. "The deal is on. And it's all for you."

"Your ship just came in, son." Lester pushed his hands deep into the pockets of his suit jacket.

Four tilted his head. "So this has nothing to do with getting my dad out of jail?"

The lawman snorted.

"We're trying to offer you the deal your daddy was too stupid to take," Deere responded, his voice almost fatherly.

His back stiffened but Four's voice remained measured. "What deal is that?"

"The one you just agreed to. Well, we have to adjust it down. I can't give you more than twenty-five percent. We offered Henry thirty-three, but then he was the grower."

". . . What was so special about that deal?"

"Protection," Deere replied. "Protection from the police, by the police. Peace of mind, all by bringing the police in as our partner."

Four gazed from Deere to Lester. "So you were in with drug boss here before my dad went to jail? Kind of makes me wonder about that good plea bargain you supposedly got for him. Still, I don't know why Dad would turn down such a surefire deal as that."

"He lost his nerve, I expect." Lester shrugged.

"Henry Truett? Lost his nerve?"

"Oh, of course that's not it, Four," Deere said. "Let's be honest here. Henry wanted out. He didn't like losing control of the operation and the way we wanted to expand it. He didn't like our new partnership. And, of course, we couldn't let him out. You understand that, don't you, Four? We aren't talking about a few hundred thousand dollars running moonshine while dodging revenuers. We're talking about seven figures every year for the rest of your life. And it's secure, because Corbin knows everything about state drug enforcement. And he's the liaison with the feds."

She saw Four jerk then, as if shocked. His gun—the Repeater he had worn on the mountain—appeared, extended and trained on the officer.

"Take your hands out of your pockets, slow." As Lester lifted his hands, Four continued, his voice low and steady. "So that's how the DEA managed to ambush my dad."

"Don't get lost in that, Four. This is business. Too much business to hold a grudge over. Nobody got killed."

"Tell that to the guys Dad shot up. And he's in jail because you guys set him up."

"A good lawyer can get him out." Deere's voice was smooth and earnest. "With the kind of money you got coming, you can hire the best lawyers in Arkansas."

He nodded. "Uh-huh. And what if I get stupid like my dad and turn down this deal?"

Deere looked down, shaking his head. "Oh don't even go there, Four."

It was then that Koral saw Lester flex his hand. It was his right hand, held part way up in respect of Four holding a gun on him. Only Four was staring at Deere, listening to him, and did not see Lester open and close his hand quickly three times.

"Don't focus on the negative, Four," Deere said. "Think about what you can do for yourself and those you care about." He paused and looked intently at Four. "Don't let yourself think about the position you put us in and what you'll force us to do."

From the corner of her eye, Koral detected motion from the Crown Vic. A figure was crouched in the front seat, slowly moving toward the open door. Koral gazed toward the slight motion. The movement stopped. Whoever it was, someone had climbed outside the car.

"What you'll be forced to do?" Four's tone was incredulous. "Has it escaped you that I'm the one holding the gun on both of you?"

She pulled the night vision goggles before her eyes, shielding them with a gloved hand from the painful brightness of the headlights, and focused on the back of the Crown Vic. A man in a police uniform crept slowly behind the car. As he drew to the passenger's side of the rear bumper and paused—pistol in hand, eyes on Four—Koral recognized him. Skyler Blank.

Deere chuckled. "Oh come on, Four. You know you're not going to hurt us. You're not that way. Why don't you just take some time—a day or two—and think this over?"

Koral remained absolutely still, watching Blank crawl toward the clearing, his path taking him between her and the Crown Vic. She was, she knew, invisible to him so long as she made no movement, or sound. As he crawled forward, he was scarcely fifteen feet from her, his eyes fixed on Four. She could see the hand that gripped his gun trembling.

"We can sweeten the deal for you, Four." Deere said, his tone almost cheerful. It was eerie to Koral. Deere knew that someone was creeping up on them and he was doing his best to keep Four distracted.

"How's that?"

"Well, take that pretty girl you've been consorting with."

Koral gasped. She wondered if Blank heard it, but he continued on. The sound of the car engine, meant to prevent Four from hearing him, prevented Blank from hearing her.

"What about her? She has nothing to do with this."

"Oh I know, Four. I know. There is no reason for her to be involved. That's why you should never have brought her on the mountain."

"You have no idea who she is. I carried her up here from New Orleans for the weekend and I already sent her—"

"Koral Walker's her name," Deere said. "Save your breath, Four. And don't think we're the only ones who know that, for goodness sake." His expression was one of mock pity. "You have so much as stake here, Four. Help us to help you."

Her heart pounded in her throat. What should she do? She couldn't shoot Blank, could she? One shot might provoke an all-out gunfight. What should she do? She lifted her goggles and watched the deputy slowly rise.

"Drop it!"

Four froze. Koral knew he recognized the officer's voice. If he turned and fired, likely he would kill the deputy. Four too was uncertain about what to do.

"Drop it or I'll shoot!"

Slowly he lowered the gun, dropped it and raised his hands.

"Skyler," Four said. "Why are you here?"

"What?"

"Did they tell you why they brought you out here tonight?"

"Go ahead, deputy," Lester said, "tell him."

"Drug sting," Blank said, his voice quivering. "Officer Lester and Mr. Deere trapped you into trying to sell your marijuana crop to him."

Four's head dropped forward.

Deere's great smile returned. "This will work out, Four. This way everybody lives. The Truetts lose the mountain but nobody gets hurt."

Lester extracted his service pistol, a .9 Glock, from his coat pocket and held it by his side. "You can live with that, can't you, son? If not, there is another way we can handle it. We can resolve everything quick, if that's your choosing and you won't go along."

The instant Four saw the red dot on Ham Deere's chest, he knew who was near. He had not known she had a laser-sighted pistol and did not know exactly what her intention was, but he knew Koral was there. And he prepared himself.

Skyler Blank saw the dot as well and it totally confused him. From six feet away, Four slipped closer to the deputy, standing only an arm's length away.

Lester saw the dot then and Deere, who did not understand why the others were staring at him, looked down at his chest. Then the tiny red circle disappeared. Blank held his service revolver toward Four. Lester raised the Glock in front of him, bracing it with both hands. He swung it around the clearing, watching for the light to reappear so he could fire at the source. And that was the motion Koral had been waiting for. An instant before the shot, she flicked the laser back on and Four saw the dot.

At the report, the Glock flew through the air; and, in the same instant, Four forced Skyler's hand upward, swept his arm around behind him and fired a shot in the dirt between Deere's feet.

For an instant no one moved.

Blank's piece trained on the others, Four spoke between ragged breaths. "On your knees. Both of you. Hands behind your head, boys."

Koral appeared, her pistol in hand, the laser target aimed at Deere. She stood beside Four, returning his gaze.

He smiled. "Black suits you."

"Just trying to be inconspicuous."

"I had this under control, you know."

"Really. I could tell."

"Nice shooting, though. Will you get Deere's gun?"

Deere shook his head. "I'm not armed. If you don't carry a gun, generally you don't get shot."

Koral kept the laser along the edges of his left eye so he would know where the bullet would go if she fired. She stepped behind him and pulled a Beretta from the little holster in the back of his pants.

"Nice weapon." She tossed it into the darkness. "Now what?"

"I'd check him for more guns and knives and whatever. And, Ham, if you move and she doesn't kill you, I will."

As she ran her left hand across his pockets and down his arms and legs, Deere whispered to her, his voice smooth and calm. "You're a pretty smart girl with some unusual talents. There's a way we can all come out on this deal, sweetie."

She pointed the laser at his crotch. "If you say one more word, I will shoot your balls off. And I can get them both with one shot."

Four lowered Skyler to the ground, face first. He pulled the handcuffs from his belt.

"Skyler, just lie here and don't move. I promise you it will be all right. And you know you can trust me."

Four stepped to Lester, who had blood running down his right wrist from his hand atop his head. Four reached beneath the man's coat and produced a second pair of handcuffs.

"That's just a through-and-through by your thumb, Corbin. Stings though, don't it?" He raised the officer to his feet and brought him over to where Deere was sitting. "Back to back, boys." He linked the handcuffs so each wore one clasp of a set and they were immobilized.

Koral and Four stood above Skyler. She held the mp3 player out, waving it before Four's eyes. Then she stooped and put her hands on the deputy's shoulders.

"Sit up, Skyler," she said. "As God is your witness, do you believe that you came here tonight to bust Four Truett for selling marijuana to Ham Deere?"

He wiped his nose on the back of his hand. "Yes. Why else?"

"Listen to this."

She began to replay the digital recorder. Skyler listened—as did the silent conspirators sitting in the dust—to the conversation that took place while he hid in the car, right up to the point when he had shouted to Four to drop his gun. His bearing changed as the recording played and he pieced together the treachery of which he had been part.

"Do you understand what they were doing?" Koral asked.

"Yeah." He nodded.

She took the mp3 player and hung it around Skyler's neck. "That's some really good detective work."

"… What?"

"Oh yeah," Four said. "That's right."

"I'm amazed at the way you figured out that a state police officer and a drug lord tried to involve you in entrapping a law-abiding citizen so they could steal his mountain to grow drugs, and how you were able to tape them implicating themselves not only in a drug conspiracy, but also in attempting to kill Henry Truett by setting him up with the DEA."

"But the best part," Four said, "was when you pulled your pistol when they resisted arrest and shot the gun right out of Lester's hand."

A strange look of possibility came over Skyler's face. He shook his head. "They'll say it never happened like that."

"Ah," Four said, "but I saw the whole thing. You're a righteous lawman, Skyler. Tonight you saved my life. You broke up a drug ring. You brought a corrupt officer to justice. As a peace officer, after tonight, you will be able to write your own ticket to any law enforcement position in our state. Not to mention that you have my eternal gratitude." Four handed the service revolver, grip first, back to Skyler.

Koral helped him to his feet. "You should go use Lester's radio to call for an ambulance and for the county sheriff and whoever else you'd like to come up here and hear the story first-hand."

"What about them?"

"Shit, Skyler," Four said. "The next talking they do will be to their attorneys."

Koral put her arms around the deputy's shoulders. "Forgive my makeup, Skyler." She kissed him. "I'm in your debt. Always."

He pursed his lips, as if holding the kiss in. Wordlessly he turned toward the Crown Vic and walked away.

Four watched him, then turned to her. "So how do we explain you? Or are you just going to hide in the bushes until everyone is gone?"

"Ha." She smiled broadly. "I'd love to stick around, but my ride is waiting."

"Oh. Well. Tell him the beer's on me."

Chapter 9

Sitting in the shady picnic area, Koral was not nearly so anxious about seeing Henry Truett the second time as she had been the first time she had visited the prison. What did make her somewhat anxious was the way Four seemed to be staring at her continually.

"Why are you looking at me like that?"

"You look really nice."

She nodded. "And that surprises you?"

"No. You always look nice. I think this is the first time I've seen you outside of the classroom when you weren't wearing jeans."

"I don't wear 'em to bed."

"Really? I got to quit turning out the lights." They laughed. "I guess I'm saying that outfit is really pretty—white blouse, matching pants. Very feminine …. You trying to impress my dad?"

She thought about it. "I already did that. Wasn't all that hard. But I am glad for him to know I'm not always butch."

"That's too bad."

"Oh?"

"I was hoping you were trying to impress me."

Her eyebrows arched. "Why would I want to do that?"

He stared at her. She stared back.

"I'm thinking."

They laughed together. She twisted girlishly on the bench beside him.

"Actually I'm scouting around for a good-looking guard. There's something about a man in uniform."

"Skyler ain't dating anybody."

She giggled and covered her mouth. "And what a good kisser he is."

". . . What he did do was a great job of was telling the police that story you made up, again and again. He must've told it six or seven times. Every time a new high-ranking state or county guy showed up, they made him tell it again. And every time he told it, he added

125

another wrinkle. I believe by now he really thinks he apprehended those two."

"Skyler lives a make-believe life anyway, doesn't he?"

Four nodded in slow agreement. "We turned him into the hero he always fantasized about being."

"Hey!"

The voice of Henry Truett startled them. He slid into the bench across the picnic table from them. His face radiated joy. And relief.

"Here you are back again, Miss Walker, brightening up our prison yard. I see you haven't been able to get shed of your stalker just yet."

"I'm so very glad to see you, too, Henry."

"Well, two visits in less than a week." He turned his attention to Four. "Something must be going on."

"We're getting you out of here, Dad."

His expression darkened. "Please tell me you aren't still thinking of dropping a dime on Ham Deere to help Corbin Lester. Please don't do that, son."

"Corbin Lester and Ham Deere are both in jail, Dad. They were in cahoots to raise weed on the mountain. But of course you know that. The first time they tried to be your partners, you said 'no'."

Henry studied his face in amazement.

"Did you also know that Lester is the one who set you up with the feds? He was really trying to get you killed."

"Well, I sort of figured that. How did you learn all this? And who busted those two bad boys?"

"Night before last up on Caddo Creek, Skyler Blank taped them and arrested 'em both."

Henry's mouth dropped. "Oh, son. For a minute there you had me going. None of this is true. You just slyly tricked me into confessing what I knew."

Four extended his hands, palms up. "As God is my witness, those two are in jail and Skyler did the arresting."

" … First off, if a big lawman like Lester and a kingpin like Deere ended up in jail, everybody in the state would know about it—especially in here. And Skyler arresting either one of them is like Barney Fife arresting John Dillinger."

"Skyler might have had some help from friends—who didn't want credit for it. And the state police are keeping a lid on this for a few days. They're up on the mountain destroying a big crop and rounding up some conspirators. When they were arrested, before the sun came up the next morning, they both cut deals. Named names."

Awe returned to Henry's face. "I'll be damned."

"All this isn't the reason we came to see you, Dad. You know the sting Lester convinced me to pull on Deere?"

Henry nodded. "It was a setup."

"Turns out the governor didn't know a thing about it. But we're still getting you out of here."

"I don't see how, son. Me shooting those DEA fellows had nothing to do with all these doings."

"Actually it does. We have 'em on tape admitting they set you up. They were trying to murder you. That invalidates your plea bargain. We've hired you a new lawyer. A good one. He says this is 'fruit of the poison tree', whatever that means. Says he'll have you out within the week."

Henry's face was full of disapproval. "You shouldn't have done that, son. You're spending money neither of us has. And these shyster lawyers are always bragging about being able to do things they really can't—"

"Mr. Truett." Koral spoke for the first time. Her voice was gentle and firm. "You should be very proud of Four."

He stared at her. He sighed at length, his face dropping.

"I am proud of him, Koral. More than I can put in words. . . . I was proud of him for enlisting to be a Marine. Proud of him for saving the lives of those fellows in Afghanistan—although I wanted to kill him myself for being so stupid." Tears began to trail down his cheeks, though his tone did not change. "Proud of him for working back to health after he got blown up. Proud of him for planting orchards on the mountain and taking good care of them."

He stopped to gather himself. She didn't look at Four—and he and Henry dared not look at each other for fear of breaking down—but she could feel how emotional he was becoming.

"I'm proud of him for going to college and learning so much and doing so well. And I'm real proud of him for getting hooked up with a fine lady such as yourself. . . . I reckon, if he gets me out of here—far-fetched as that is—I'll have even more reason to be proud."

He leaned forward, studying the picnic table. "Now me, on the other hand, every day I'm in here is another reminder of what a failure I am. In so many ways. I guess I push old Four so he keeps going in the direction he's going, so he don't end up like me."

"No, Henry," Koral said. "You are not in the prison because you are a bad person. You're here because you refused to do something you thought was wrong. We heard Mr. Deere say that you refused to enter a big conspiracy with him and Mr. Lester and that they couldn't let you get by with that. That's how Four knew they set you up—and they pretty much admitted it."

Henry, eyes wide, looked at his son. "She was there?"

Four nodded. "Wasn't my doing. She crashed the party. Thank God."

"And the whole reason you were in that shoot-out was because of their treachery. That was self-defense. You shouldn't have been here in the first place. Well, not for that. I'm not saying it's okay to raise and sell marijuana. At least not in Arkansas."

As he gazed at her, a broad smile spread slowly across his face. "You are one amazing young woman."

"Let me tell you about her, Dad. She's so smart and so good. I have no idea what she sees in me, but I'm hanging onto her as long as I can. I love her, Dad. I'm crazy about her."

Koral felt her face grow hot and the tears, irresistible, began. "That's the first time he's said he loved me."

Henry nodded. "He was just waiting for a real romantic setting, like the jail house."

"She's been trying to fix me, Dad. And I'm going to let her."

www.ingramcontent.com/pod-product-compliance
Lightning Source LLC
Chambersburg PA
CBHW070339130626
46556CB00007B/2935